Richard Carvel.
Volume 6

by Winston Churchill

Title: Richard Carvel, Volume 6
Author: Winston Churchill
Language: English

RICHARD CARVEL

By Winston Churchill

Volume 6.

XXXIV. His Grace makes Advances
XXXV. In which my Lord Baltimore appears
XXXVI. A Glimpse of Mr. Garrick
XXXVII. The Serpentine
XXXVIII. In which I am roundly brought to task
XXXIX. Holland House
XL. Vauxhall

CHAPTER XXXIV

HIS GRACE MAKES ADVANCES

The next morning I began casting about as to what I should do next. There was no longer any chance of getting at the secret from Dorothy, if secret there were. Whilst I am ruminating comes a great battling at the street door, and Jack Comyn blew in like a gust of wind, rating me soundly for being a lout and a blockhead.

"Zooks!" he cried, "I danced the soles off my shoes trying to get in here yesterday, and I hear you were moping all the time, and paid me no more attention than I had been a dog scratching at the door. What! and have you fallen out with my lady?"

I confessed the whole matter to him. He was not to be resisted. He called to Banks for a cogue of Nantsey, and swore amazingly at what he was pleased to term the inscrutability of woman, offering up consolation by the wholesale. The incident, he said, but strengthened his conviction that Mr. Manners had appealed to Dorothy to save him. "And then," added his Lordship, facing me with absolute fierceness, "and then, Richard, why the devil did she weep? There were no tears when I made my avowal. I tell you, man, that the whole thing points but the one way. She loves you. I swear it by the rood."

I could not help laughing, and he stood looking at me with such a whimsical expression that I rose and flung my arms around him.

"Jack, Jack!" I cried, "what a fraud you are! Do you remember the argument you used when you had got me out of the sponging-house? Quoting you, all I had to do was to put Dorothy to the proof, and she would toss Mr. Marmaduke and his honour broadcast. Now I have confessed myself, and what is the result? Nay, your theory is gone up in vapour."

"Then why," cried his Lordship, hotly, "why before refusing me did she demand to know whether you had been in love with Patty Swain? 'Sdeath! you put me in mind of a woman upon stilts —a man has always to be walking alongside her with encouragement handy. And when a proud creature such as our young lady breaks down as she hath done, 'tis clear as skylight there is something wrong. And as for Mr. Manners, Hare overheard a part of a pow-wow 'twixt him and the duke at the Bedford Arms,—and Chartersea has all but owned in some of his drunken fits that our little fop is in his power."

"Then she is in love with some one else," I said.

"I tell you she is not," said Comyn, still more emphatically; "and you can write that down in red in your table book. Gossip has never been able to connect her name with that of any man save yours, when she went for you in Castle Yard. And, gemini, gossip is like water, and will get in if a crack shows. When the Marquis of Wells was going to Arlington Street once every day, she sent him about his business in a fortnight."

Despite Comyn's most unselfish optimism, I

could see no light. And in the recklessness that so often besets youngsters of my temper, on like occasions, I went off to Newmarket next day with Mr. Fox and Lord Ossory, in his Lordship's travelling-chaise and four. I spent a very gay week trying to forget Miss Dolly. I was the loser by some three hundred pounds, in addition to what I expended and loaned to Mr. Fox. This young gentleman was then beginning to accumulate at Newmarket a most execrable stud. He lost prodigiously, but seemed in no wise disturbed thereby. I have never known a man who took his ill-luck with such a stoical nonchalance. Not so while the heat was on. As I write, a most ridiculous recollection rises of Charles dragging his Lordship and me and all who were with him to that part of the course where the race was highest, where he would act like a madman; blowing and perspiring, and whipping and swearing all at a time, and rising up and down as if the horse was throwing him.

At Newmarket I had the good—or ill-fortune to meet that incorrigible rake and profligate, my Lord of March and Ruglen. For him the goddess of Chance had smiled, and he was in the most complaisant humour. I was presented to his Grace, the Duke of Grafton, whose name I had no reason to love, and invited to Wakefield Lodge. We went instead, Mr. Fox and I, to Ampthill, Lord Ossory's seat, with a merry troop. And then we had more racing; and whist and quinze and pharaoh and hazard, until I was obliged to write another draft upon Mr. Dix to settle the wails: and picquet in the travelling-chaise all the way to London. Dining at

Brooks's, we encountered Fitzpatrick and Comyn and my Lord Carlisle.

"Now how much has Charles borrowed of you, Mr. Carvel?" demanded
Fitzpatrick, as we took our seats.

"I'll lay ten guineas that Charles has him mortgaged this day month, though he owns as much land as William Penn, and is as rich as Fordyce."

Comyn demanded where the devil I had been, though he knew perfectly. He was uncommonly silent during dinner, and then asked me if I had heard the news. I told him I had heard none. He took me by the sleeve, to the quiet amusement of the company, and led me aside.

"Curse you, Richard," says be; "you have put me in such a temper that I vow I'll fling you over. You profess to love her, and yet you go betting to Newmarket and carousing to Ampthill when she is ill."

"Ill!" I said, catching my breath.

"Ay! That hurts, does it? Yes, ill, I say. She was missed at Lady
Pembroke's that Friday you had the scene with her, and at Lady
Ailesbury's on Saturday. On Monday morning, when I come to you for
tidings, you are off watching Charles make an ass of himself at
Newmarket."

"And how is she now, Comyn?" I asked, catching him by the arm.

"You may go yourself and see, and be cursed,

Richard Carvel. She is in trouble, and you are pleasure-seeking in the country. Damme! you deserve richly to lose her."

Calling for my greatcoat, and paying no heed to the jeers of the company for leaving before the toasts and the play, I fairly ran to Arlington Street. I was in a passion of remorse. Comyn had been but just. Granting, indeed, that she had refused to marry me, was that any reason why I should desert my life-long friend and playmate? A hundred little tokens of her affection for me rose to mind, and last of all that rescue from Castle Yard in the face of all Mayfair. And in that hour of darkness the conviction that something was wrong came back upon me with redoubled force. Her lack of colour, her feverish actions, and the growing slightness of her figure, all gave me a pang, as I connected them with that scene on the balcony over the Park.

The house was darkened, and a coach was in front of it.

"Yessir," said the footman, "Miss Manners has been quite ill. She is now some better, and Dr. James is with her. Mrs. Manners begs company will excuse her."

And Mr. Marmaduke? The man said, with as near a grin as he ever got, that the marster was gone to Mrs. Cornelys's assembly. As I turned away, sick at heart, the physician, in his tie-wig and scarlet cloak, came out, and I stopped him. He was a testy man, and struck the stone an impatient blow with his staff.

"'Od's life, sir. I am besieged day and night by you young gentlemen.

I begin to think of sending a daily card to Almack's."

"Sir, I am an old friend of Miss Manners," I replied, "having grown up with her in Maryland—"

"Are you Mr. Carvel?" he demanded abruptly, taking his hat from his arm.

"Yes," I answered, surprised. In the gleam of the portico lanthorn he scrutinized me for several seconds.

"There are some troubles of the mind which are beyond the power of physic to remedy, Mr. Carvel," said he. "She has mentioned your name, sir, and you are to judge of my meaning. Your most obedient, sir. Good night, sir."

And he got into his coach, leaving me standing where I was, bewildered.

That same fear of being alone, which has driven many a man to his cups, sent me back to Brooks's for company. I found Fox and Comyn seated at a table in the corner of the drawing-room, for once not playing, but talking earnestly. Their expressions when they saw me betrayed what my own face must have been.

"What is it?" cried Comyn, half rising; "is she —is she—"

"No, she is better," I said.

He looked relieved.

"You must have frightened him badly, Jack," said Fox.

I flung myself into a chair, and Fox proposed whist, something unusual for him. Comyn called for cards, and was about to go in search of a fourth, when we all three caught sight of the Duke of

Chartersea in the door, surveying the room with a cold leisure. His eye paused when in line with us, and we were seized with astonishment to behold him making in our direction.

"Squints!" exclaimed Mr. Fox, "now what the devil can the hound want?"

"To pull your nose for sending him to market," my Lord suggested.

Fox laughed coolly.

"Lay you twenty he doesn't, Jack," he said.

His Grace plainly had some business with us, and I hoped he was coming to force the fighting. The pieces had ceased to rattle on the round mahogany table, and every head in the room seemed turned our way, for the Covent Garden story was well known. Chartersea laid his hand on the back of our fourth chair, greeted us with some ceremony, and said something which, under the circumstances, was almost unheard of in that day: "If you stand in need of one, gentlemen, I should deem it an honour."

The situation had in it enough spice for all of us. We welcomed him with alacrity. The cards were cut, and it fell to his Grace to deal, which he did very prettily, despite his heavy hands. He drew Charles Fox, and they won steadily. The conversation between deals was anywhere; on the virtue of Morello cherries for the gout, to which his Grace was already subject; on Mr. Fox's Ariel, and why he had not carried Sandwich's cup at Newmarket; on the advisability of putting three-year-olds on the track; in short, on a dozen small topics of the kind. At length, when Comyn and I had lost some fifty pounds between us, Chartersea threw down the cards.

"My coach waits to-night, gentlemen," said he, with some sort of an accent that did not escape us. "It would give me the greatest pleasure and you will sup with me in Hanover Square."

CHAPTER XXXV

IN WHICH MY LORD BALTIMORE APPEARS

His Grace's offer was accepted with a readiness he could scarce have expected, and we all left the room in the midst of a buzz of comment. We knew well that the matter was not so haphazard as it appeared, and on the way to Hanover Square Comyn more than once steppcd on my toe, and I answered the pressure. Our coats and canes were taken by the duke's lackeys when we arrived. We were shown over the house. Until now —so his Grace informed us—it had not been changed since the time of the fourth duke, who, as we doubtless knew, had been an ardent supporter of the Hanoverian succession. The rooms were high-panelled and furnished in the German style, as was the fashion when the Square was built. But some were stripped and littered with scaffolding and plaster, new and costly marble mantels were replacing the wood, and an Italian of some renown was decorating the ceilings. His Grace appeared to be at some pains that the significance of these improvements should not be lost upon us; was constantly appealing to Mr. Fox's taste on this or that feature. But those fishy eyes of his were so alert that we had not even opportunity to wink. It was wholly patent, in brief, that the Duke of Chartersea meant to be married, and had brought Charles and Comyn hither with a purpose. For me he would have put himself out not an inch had he not understood that my support came from those quarters.

He tempered off this exhibition by showing us a collection of pottery famous in England, that had belonged to the fifth duke, his father. Every piece of it, by the way, afterwards brought an enormous sum at auction. Supper was served in a warm little room of oak. The game was from Derresley Manor, the duke's Nottinghamshire seat, and the wine, so he told us, was some of fifty bottles of rare Chinon he had inherited. Melted rubies it was indeed, of the sort which had quickened the blood of many a royal gathering at Blois and Amboise and Chenonceaux, —the distilled peasant song of the Loire valley. In it many a careworn clown had tasted the purer happiness of the lowly. Our restraint gave way under its influence. His Grace lost for the moment his deformities, and Mr. Fox made us laugh until our sides ached again. His Lordship told many a capital yarn, and my own wit was afterwards said to be astonishing, though I can recall none of it to support the affirmation.

Not a word or even a hint of Dorothy had been uttered, nor did Chartersea so much as refer to his Covent Garden experience. At length, when some half dozen of the wine was gone, and the big oak clock had struck two, the talk lapsed. It was Charles Fox, of course, who threw the spark into the powder box.

"We were speaking of hunting, Chartersea," he said. "Did you ever know
George Wrottlesey, of the Suffolk branch?"

"No," said his Grace, very innocent.

"No! 'Od's whips and spurs, I'll be sworn I never saw a man to beat him for reckless riding. He would take five bars any time, egad, and sit any colt that was ever foaled. The Wrottleseys were poor as weavers then, with the Jews coming down in the wagon from London and hanging round the hall gates. But the old squire had plenty of good hunters in the stables, and haunches on the board, and a cellar that was like the widow's cruse of oil, or barrel of meal—or whatever she had. All the old man had to do to lose a guinea was to lay it on a card. He never nicked in his life, so they say. Well, young George got after a rich tea-merchant's daughter who had come into the country near by. 'Slife! she was a saucy jade, and devilish pretty. Such a face! so Stavordale vowed, and such a neck! and such eyes! so innocent, so ravishingly innocent. But she knew cursed well George was after the bank deposit, and kept him galloping. And when he got a view, halloa, egad! she was stole away again, and no scent.

"One morning George was out after the hounds with Stavordale, who told me the story, and a lot of fellows who had come over from Newmarket. He was upon Aftermath, the horse that Foley bought for five hundred pounds and was a colt then. Of course he left the field out of sight behind. He made for a gap in the park wall (faith! there was no lack of 'em), but the colt refused, and over went George and plumped into a cart of winter apples some farmer's sot was taking to Bury Saint Edmunds to market. The fall knocked the sense out of George, for he hasn't much, and Stavordale thinks he must have struck a stake as he went in. Anyway, the apples rolled over on top of him, and the drunkard on the seat never woke up, i' faith. And so they came to town.

"It so chanced, egad, that the devil sent Miss Tea Merchant to Bury to buy apples. She amused herself at playing country gentlewoman while papa worked all week in the city. She saw the cart in the market, and ate three (for she had the health of a barmaid), and bid in the load, and George with it. 'Pon my soul! she did. They found his boots first. And the lady said, before all the grinning Johns and Willums, that since she had bought him she supposed she would have to keep him. And, by Gads life! she has got him yet, which is a deal stranger."

Even the duke laughed. For, as Fox told it, the story was irresistible. But it came as near to being a wanton insult as a reference to his Grace's own episode might. The red came slowly back into his eye. Fox stared vacantly, as was his habit when he had done or said something especially daring. And Comyn and I waited, straining and expectant, like boys who have prodded a wild beast and stand ready for the spring. There was a metallic ring in the duke's voice as he spoke.

"I have heard, Mr. Carvel, that you can ride any mount offered you."

"Od's, and so he can!" cried Jack. "I'll take oath on that."

"I will lay you an hundred guineas, my Lord," says his Grace, very off-hand, "that Mr. Carvel does not sit Baltimore's Pollux above twenty minutes."

"Done!" says Jack, before I could draw breath.

"I'll take your Grace for another hundred," calmly added Mr. Fox.

"It seems to me, your Grace," I cried, angry all at once, "it seems to me that I am the one to whom you should address your wagers. I am not a jockey, to be put up at your whim, and to give you the chance to lose money."

Chartersea swung around my way.

"Your pardon, Mr. Carvel," said he, very coolly, very politely; "yours is the choice of the wager. And you reject it, the others must be called off."

"Slife! I double it!" I said hotly, "provided the horse is alive, and will stand up."

"Devilish well put, Richard!" Mr. Fox exclaimed, casting off his restraint.

"I give you my word the horse is alive, sir," he answered, with a mock bow; "'twas only yesterday that he killed his groom, at Hampstead."

A few moments of silence followed this

revelation. It was Charles Fox who spoke first.

"I make no doubt that your Grace, as a man of honour,"—he emphasized the word forcibly, —"will not refuse to ride the horse for another twenty minutes, provided Mr. Carvel is successful. And I will lay your Grace another hundred that you are thrown, or run away with."

Truly, to cope with a wit like Mr. Fox's, the duke had need for a longer head. He grew livid as he perceived how neatly he had been snared in his own trap.

"Done!" he cried loudly; "done, gentlemen. It only remains to hit upon time and place for the contest. I go to York to-morrow, to be back this day fortnight. And if you will do me the favour of arranging with Baltimore for the horse, I shall be obliged. I believe he intends selling it to Astley, the showman."

"And are we to keep it?" asks Mr. Fox.

"I am dealing with men of honour," says the duke, with a bow: "I need have no better assurance that the horse will not be ridden in the interval."

"'Od so!" said Comyn, when we were out; "very handsome of him. But I would not say as much for his Grace."

And Mr. Fox declared that the duke was no coward, but all other epithets known might be called him. "A very diverting evening, Richard," said he; "let's to your apartments and have a bowl, and talk it over."

And thither we went.

I did not sleep much that night, but 'twas of Dolly I thought rather than of Chartersea. I was abroad early, and over to inquire in Arlington Street, where I found she had passed a good night. And I sent Banks a-hooting for some violets to send her, for I knew she loved that flower.

Between ten and eleven Mr. Fox and Comyn and I set out for Baltimore House. When you go to London, my dears, you will find a vast difference in the neighbourhood of Bloomsbury from what it was that May morning in 1770. Great Russell Street was all a sweet fragrance of gardens, mingling with the smell of the fields from the open country to the north. We drove past red Montagu House with its stone facings and dome, like a French hotel, and the cluster of buildings at its great gate. It had been then for over a decade the British Museum. The ground behind it was a great resort for Londoners of that day. Many a sad affair was fought there, but on that morning we saw a merry party on their way to play prisoner's base.

Then we came to the gardens in front of Bedford House, which are now Bloomsbury Square. For my part I preferred this latter mansion to the French creation by its side, and admired its long and graceful lines. Its windows commanded a sweep from Holborn on the south to Highgate on the north. To the east of it, along Southampton Row, a few great houses had gone up or were building; and at the far end of that was Baltimore house, overlooking her Grace of Bedford's gardens. Beyond Lamb's Conduit Fields stretched away to the countryside.

I own I had a lively curiosity to see that lordly ruler, the proprietor of our province, whose birthday we celebrated after his Majesty's. Had I not been in a great measure prepared, I should have had a revulsion indeed.

When he heard that Mr. Fox and my Lord Comyn were below stairs he gave orders to show them up to his bedroom, where he received us in a night-gown embroidered with oranges. My Lord Baltimore, alas! was not much to see. He did not make the figure a ruler should as he sat in his easy chair, and whined and cursed his Swiss. He was scarce a year over forty, and he had all but run his race. Dissipation and corrosion had set their seal upon him, had stamped his yellow face with crows' feet and blotted it with pimples. But then the glimpse of a fine gentleman just out of bed of a morning, before he is made for the day, is unfair.

"Morning, Charles! Howdy, Jack!" said his Lordship, apathetically. "Glad to know you, Mr. Carvel. Heard of your family. 'Slife! Wish there were more like 'em in the province."

This sentiment not sitting very well upon his Lordship, I bowed, and said nothing.

"By the bye," he continued, pouring out his chocolate into the dish, "I sent a damned rake of a parson out there some years gone. Handsome devil, too. Never seen his match with the women, egad. 'Od's fish—" he leered. And then added with an oath and a nod and a vile remark: "Married three times to my knowledge. Carried off dozen or so more. Some of 'em for me. Many a good night I've had with him. Drank between us one evening at Essex's gallon and half Champagne and Burgundy apiece. He got to know too much, y' know," he concluded, with a wicked wink. "Had to buy him up pack him off."

"His name, Fred?" said Comyn, with a smile at me.

"'Sdeath! That's it. Trouble to remember. Damned if I can think." And he repeated this remark over and over.

"Allen?" said Comyn.

"Yes," said Baltimore; "Allen. And egad I think he'll find hell a hotter place than me. You know him, Mr. Carvel?"

"Yes," I replied. I said no more. I make no reservations when I avow I was never so disgusted in my life. But as I looked upon him, haggard and worn, with retribution so neat at hand, I had no words to protest or condemn.

Baltimore gave a hollow mirthless laugh, stopped short, and looked at
Charles Fox.

"Curse you, Charles! I suppose you are after that little matter I owe you for quinze."

"Damn the little matter!" said Fox. "Come, get you perfumed and dressed,
and order up some of your Tokay while we wait. I have to go to St.
Stephens. Mr. Carvel has come to buy your horse Pollux. He has bet
Chartersea two hundred guineas he rides him for twenty minutes."

"The devil he has!" cried his Lordship, jaded no longer. "Why, you must know, Mr. Carvel, there was no groom in my stables who would sit him until Foley made me a present of his man, Miller, who started to ride him to Hyde Park. As he came out of Great Russell Street, by gads life! the horse broke and ran out the Tottenham Court Road all the way to Hampstead. And the fiend picked out a big stone water trough and tossed Miller against it. Then they gathered up the fragments. Damme if I like to see suicide, Mr. Carvel. If Chartersea wants to kill you, let him try it in the fields behind Montagu House here."

I told his Lordship that I had made the wager, and could not in honour withdraw, though the horse had killed a dozen grooms. But already he seemed to have lost interest. He gave a languid pull at the velvet tassel on his bell-rope, ordered the wine; and, being informed that his anteroom below was full of people, had them all dismissed with the message that he was engaged upon important affairs. He told Mr. Fox he had heard of the Jerusalem Chamber, and vowed he would have a like institution. He told me he wished the colony of Maryland in hell; that he was worn out with the quarrels of Governor Eden and his Assembly, and offered to lay a guinea that the Governor's agent would get to him that day,—will-he, nill-he. I did not think it worth while to argue with such a man.

My Lord took three-quarters of an hour to dress, and swore he had not accomplished the feat so quickly in a year. He washed his hands and face in a silver basin, and the scent of the soap filled the room. He rated his Swiss for putting cinnamon upon his ruffles in place of attar of roses, and attempted to regale us the while with some of his choicest adventures. In more than one of these, by the way, his Grace of Chartersea figured. It was Fox who brought him up.

"See here, Baltimore," he said, "I'm not squeamish. But I'm cursed if I like to hear a man who may die any time between bottles talk so."

His Lordship took the rebuke with an oath, and presently hobbled down the stairs of the great and silent house to the stable court, where two grooms were in waiting with the horse. He was an animal of amazing power, about sixteen hands, and dapple gray in colour. And it required no special knowledge to see that he had a devil inside him. It gleamed wickedly out of his eye.

"'Od's life, Richard!" cried Charles, "he has a Jew nose; by all the seven tribes I bid you 'ware of him."

"You have but to ride him with a gold bit, Richard," said Comyn, "and he is a kitten, I'll warrant."

At that moment Pollux began to rear and kick, so that it took both the 'ostlers to hold him.

"Show him a sovereign," suggested Fox. "How do you feel, Richard?"

"I never feared a horse yet," I said with perfect truth, "nor do I fear this one, though I know he may kill me."

"I'll lay you twenty pounds you have at least one bone broken, and ten that you are killed," Baltimore puts in querulously, from the doorway.

"I'll do this, my Lord," I answered. "If I ride him, he is mine. If he throws me, I give you twenty pounds for him."

The gentlemen laughed, and Baltimore vowed

he could sell the horse to Astley for fifty; that Pollux was the son of Renown, of the Duke of Kingston's stud, and much more. But Charles rallied him out by a reference to the debt at quinze, and an appeal to his honour as a sportsman. And swore he was discouraging one of the prettiest encounters that would take place in England for many a long day. And so the horse was sent to the stables of the White Horse Cellar, in Piccadilly, and left there at my order.

CHAPTER XXXVI

A GLIMPSE OF MR. GARRICK

Day after day I went to Arlington Street, each time to be turned away with the same answer: that Miss Manners was a shade better, but still confined to her bed. You will scarce believe me, my dears, when I say that Mr. Marmaduke had gone at this crisis with his Grace to the York races. On the fourth morning, I think, I saw Mrs. Manners. She was much worn with the vigil she had kept, and received me with an apathy to frighten me. Her way with me had hitherto always been one of kindness and warmth. In answer to the dozen questions I showered upon her, she replied that Dorothy's malady was in no wise dangerous, so Dr. James had said, and undoubtedly arose out of the excitement of a London season. As I knew, Dorothy was of the kind that must run and run until she dropped. She had no notion of the measure of her own strength. Mrs. Manners hoped that, in a fortnight, she would be recovered sufficiently to be removed to one of the baths.

"She wishes me to thank you for the flowers, Richard. She has them constantly by her. And bids me tell you how sorry she is that she is compelled to miss so much of your visit to England. Are you enjoying London, Richard? I hear that you are well liked by the best of company."

I left, prodigiously cast down, and went directly to Mr. Wedgwood's, to choose the prettiest set of tea-cups and dishes I could find there. I pitied Mrs. Manners from my heart, and made every allowance for her talk with me, knowing the sorrow of her life. Here was yet another link in the chain of the Chartersea evidence. And I made no doubt that Mr. Manner's brutal desertion at such a time must be hard to bear. I continued my visits of inquiry, nearly always meeting some person of consequence, or the footman of such, come on the same errand as myself. And once I encountered the young man she had championed against his Grace at Lady Tankerville's.

Rather than face the array of anxieties that beset me, I plunged recklessly into the gayeties— nay, the excesses—of Mr. Charles Fox and his associates. I paid, in truth, a very high price for my friendship with Mr. Fox. But, since it did not quite ruin me, I look back upon it as cheaply bought. To know the man well, to be the subject of his regard, was to feel an infatuation in common with the little band of worshippers which had come with him from Eton. They remained faithful to him all his days, nor adversity nor change of opinion could shake their attachment. They knew his faults, deplored them, and paid for them. And this was not beyond my comprehension, tho' many have wondered at it. Did he ask me for five hundred pounds,—which he did,—I gave it freely, and would gladly have given more, tho' I saw it all wasted in a night when the dice rolled against him. For those honoured few of whom I speak likewise knew his virtues, which were quite as large as the faults, albeit so mingled with them that all might not distinguish.

I attended some of the routs and parties, to all of which, as a young colonial gentleman of wealth and family, I was made welcome. I went to a ball at Lord Stanley's, a mixture of French horns and clarionets and coloured glass lanthorns and candles in gilt vases, and young ladies pouring tea in white, and musicians in red, and draperies and flowers ad libitum. There I met Mr. Walpole, looking on very critically. He was the essence of friendliness, asked after my equerry, and said I had done well to ship him to America. At the opera, with Lord Ossory and Mr. Fitzpatrick, I talked through the round of the boxes, from Lady Pembroke's on the right to Lady Hervey's on the left, where Dolly's illness and Lady Harrington's snuffing gabble were the topics rather than Giardini's fiddling. Mr. Storer took me to Foote's dressing-room at the Haymarket, where we found the Duke of Cumberland lounging. I was presented, and thought his Royal Highness had far less dignity than the monkey-comedian we had come to see.

I must not forget the visit I made to Drury Lane Playhouse with my Lords Carlisle and Grantham and Comyn. The great actor received me graciously in such a company, you may be sure. He appeared much smaller off the boards than on, and his actions and speech were quick and nervous. Gast, his hairdresser, was making him up for the character of Richard III.

"'Ods!" said Mr. Garrick, "your Lordships come five minutes too late.
Goldsmith is but just gone hence, fresh from his tailor, Filby, of Water
Lane. The most gorgeous creature in London, gentlemen, I'll be sworn.
He is even now, so he would have me know, gone by invitation to my Lord
Denbigh's box, to ogle the ladies."

"And have you seen your latest lampoon, Mr. Garrick?" asks Comyn, winking at me.

Up leaps Mr. Garrick, so suddenly as to knock the paint-pot from Gast's hand.

"Nay, your Lordship jests, surely!" he cried, his voice shaking.

"Jests!" says my Lord, very serious; "do I jest, Carlisle?" And turning to Mr. Cross, the prompter, who stood by, "Fetch me the St. James's Evening Post," says he.

"'Ods my life!" continues poor Garrick, almost

in tears; "I have loaned Foote upwards of two thousand pounds. And last year, as your Lordship remembers, took charge of his theatre when his leg was cut off. 'Pon my soul, I cannot account for his ingratitude."

"'Tis not Foote," says Carlisle, biting his lip; "I know Foote's mark."

"Then Johnson," says the actor, "because I would not let him have my fine books in his dirty den to be kicked about the floor, but put my library at his disposal—"

"Nay, nor Johnson. Nor yet Macklin nor Murphy."

"Surely not—" cries Mr. Garrick, turning white under the rouge. The name remained unpronounced.

"Ay, ay, Junius, in the Evening Post. He has fastened upon you at last," answers Comyn, taking the paper.

"'Sdeath! Garrick," Carlisle puts in, very solemn, "what have you done to offend the Terrible Unknown? Talebearing to his Majesty, I'll warrant! I gave you credit for more discretion."

At these words Mr. Garrick seized the chair for support, and swung heavily into it. Whereat the young lords burst into such a tempest of laughter that I could not refrain from joining them. As for Mr. Garrick, he was so pleased to have escaped that he laughed too, though with a palpable nervousness.

[Note by the editor. It was not long after this that Mr. Garrick's punishment came, and for the self-same offence.]

"By the bye, Garrick," Carlisle remarked slyly, when he had recovered, "Mrs. Crewe was vastly taken with the last 'vers' you left on her dressing-table."

"Was she, now, my Lord?" said the great actor, delighted, but scarce over his fright. "You must know that I have writ one to my Lady Carlisle, on the occasion of her dropping her fan in Piccadilly." Whereupon he proceeded to recite it, and my Lord Carlisle, being something of a poet himself, pronounced it excellent.

Mr. Garrick asked me many questions concerning American life and manners, having a play in his repertory the scene of which was laid in New York. In the midst of this we were interrupted by a dirty fellow who ran in, crying excitedly:

"Sir, the Archbishop of York is getting drunk at the Bear, and swears he'll be d——d if he'll act to-night."

"The archbishop may go to the devil!" snapped Mr. Garrick. "I do not know a greater rascal, except yourself."

I was little short of thunderstruck. But presently Mr. Garrick added complainingly:

"I paid a guinea for the archbishop, but the fellow got me three murderers to-day and the best alderman I ever clapped eyes upon. So we are square."

After the play we supped with him at his new house in Adelphi Terrace, next Topham Beauclerk's. 'Twas handsomely built in the Italian style, and newly furnished throughout, for Mr. Garrick travelled now with a coach and six and four menservants, forsooth. And amongst other things he took pride in showing us that night was a handsome snuffbox which the King of Denmark had given him the year before, his Majesty's portrait set in jewels thereon.

Presently the news of the trial of Lord Baltimore's horse began to be noised about, and was followed by a deluge of wagers at Brooks's and White's and elsewhere. Comyn and Fox, my chief supporters, laid large sums upon me, despite all my persuasion. But the most unpleasant part of the publicity was the rumour that the match was connected with the struggle for Miss Manners's hand. I was pressed with invitations to go into the country to ride this or that horse. His Grace the Duke of Grafton had a mount he would have me try at Wakefield Lodge, and was far from pleasant over my refusal of his invitation. I was besieged by young noblemen like Lord Derby and Lord Foley, until I was heartily sick of notoriety, and cursed the indiscretion of the person who let out the news, and my own likewise. My Lord March, who did me the honour to lay one hundred pounds upon my skill, insisted that I should make one of a party to the famous amphitheatre near Lambeth. Mr. Astley, the showman, being informed of his Lordship's intention, met us on Westminster Bridge dressed in his uniform as sergeant major of the Royal Light Dragoons and mounted on a white charger. He escorted us to one of the large boxes under the pent-house reserved for the gentry. And when the show was over and the place cleared, begged, that I would ride his Indian Chief. I refused; but March pressed me, and Comyn declared he had staked his reputation upon my horsemanship. Astley was a large man, about my build, and I donned a pair of his leather breeches and boots, and put Indian Chief to his paces around the ring. I found him no more restive, nor as much so, as Firefly. The gentlemen were good enough to clap me roundly, and Astley vowed (no doubt because of the noble patrons present) that he had never seen a better seat.

We all repaired afterwards for supper to Don Saltero's Coffee House and Museum in Chelsea. And I remembered having heard my grandfather speak of the place, and tell how he had seen Sir Richard Steele there, listening to the Don scraping away at the "Merry Christ Church Bells" on his fiddle. The Don was since dead, but King James's coronation sword and King Henry VIII.'s coat of mail still hung on the walls.

The remembrance of that fortnight has ever been an appalling one. Mr. Carvel had never attempted to teach me the value of money. My grandfather, indeed, held but four things essential to the conduct of life; namely, to fear God, love the King, pay your debts, and pursue your enemies. There was no one in London to advise me, Comyn being but a wild lad like myself. But my Lord Carlisle gave me a friendly warning:

"Have a care, Carvel," said he, kindly, "or you will run your grandfather through, and all your relations beside. I little realized the danger of it when I first came up." (He was not above two and twenty then.) "And now I have a wife, am more crippled than I care to be, thanks to this devilish high play. Will you dine with Lady Carlisle in St. James's Place next Friday?"

My heart went out to this young nobleman. Handsome he was, as a picture. And he knew better than most of your fine gentlemen how to put a check on his inclinations. As a friend he had few equals, his purse being ever at the command of those he loved. And his privations on Fox's account were already greater than many knew.

I had a call, too, from Mr. Dix. I found him in my parlour one morning, cringing and smiling, and, as usual, half an hour away from his point.

"I warrant you, Mr. Carvel," says he, "there are few young gentlemen not born among the elect that make the great friends you are blessed with."

"I have been fortunate, Mr. Dix," I replied dryly.

"Fortunate!" he cried; "good Lord, sir! I hear of you everywhere with Mr. Fox, and you have been to Astley's with my Lord March. And I have a draft from you at Ampthill."

"Vastly well manoeuvred, Mr. Dix," I said, laughing at the guilty change in his pink complexion. "And hence you are here."

He fidgeted, and seeing that I paid him no attention, but went on with my chocolate, he drew a paper from his pocket and opened it.

"You have spent a prodigious sum, sir, for so short a time," said he, unsteadily. "'Tis very well for you, Mr. Carvel, but I have to remember that you are heir only. I am advancing you money without advices from his Worship, your grandfather. A most irregular proceeding, sir, and one likely to lead me to trouble. I know not what your allowance may be."

"Nor I, Mr. Dix," I replied, unreasonably enough. "To speak truth, I have never had one. You have my Lord Comyn's signature to protect you," I went on ill-naturedly, for I had not had enough sleep. "And in case Mr. Carvel protests, which is unlikely and preposterous, you shall have ten percentum on your money until I can pay you. That should be no poor investment."

He apologized. But he smoothed out the paper on his knee.

"It is only right to tell you, Mr. Carvel, that you have spent one thousand eight hundred and thirty-seven odd pounds, in home money, which is worth more than your colonial. Your grandfather's balance with me was something less than one thousand five hundred, as I made him a remittance in December last. I have advanced the rest. And yesterday," he went on, resolutely for him, "yesterday I got an order for five hundred more."

And he handed me the paper. I must own that the figures startled me.
I laid it down with a fine show of indifference.

"And so you wish me to stop drawing? Very good, Mr. Dix."

He must have seen some threat implied, though I meant none. He was my very humble servant at once, and declared he had called only to let me know where I stood. Then he bowed himself out, wishing me luck with the horse he had heard of, and I lighted my pipe with his accompt.

CHAPTER XXXVII

THE SERPENTINE

Whether it was Mr. Dix. that started me reflecting, or my Lord Carlisle's warning, or a few discreet words from young Lady Carlisle herself, I know not. At all events, I made a resolution to stop high play, and confine myself to whist and quinze and picquet. For I conceived a notion, enlarged by Mr. Fox, that I had more than once fallen into the tender clutches of the hounds. I was so reflecting the morning following Lord Carlisle's dinner, when Banks announced a footman.

"Mr. Manners's man, sir," he added significantly, and handed me a little note. I seized it, and, to hide my emotion, told him to give the man his beer.

The writing was Dorothy's, and some time passed after I had torn off the wrapper before I could compose myself to read it.

"So, Sir, the Moment I am too ill to watch you you must needs lapse into Wilde & Flity Doings, for thus y'rs are call'd even in London. Never Mind how y'r Extravigancies are come to my Ears Sir. One Matter I have herd that I am Most Concerned about, & I pray you, my Dear Richard do not allow y'r Recklessness & Contemt for Danger to betray you into a Stil more Amazing Follie or I shall be very Miserable Indeed. I have Hopes that the Report is at Best a Rumour & you must sit down & write me that it is Sir that my Minde may be set at

Rest. I fear for you Vastly & I beg you not Riske y'r Life Foolishly & this for the Sake of one who subscribes herself y'r Old Playmate & Well-Wisher Dolly.

"P.S. I have writ Sir Jon Fielding to put you in the Marshallsee or New Gate until Mr. Carvel can be tolde. I am Better & hope soon to see you agen & have been informed of y'r Dayly Visitts & y'r Flowers are beside me. D. M."

In about an hour and a half, Mr. Marmaduke's footman was on his way back to Arlington Street in a condition not to be lightly spoken of. During that period I had committed an hundred silly acts, and incidentally learned the letter by heart. I was much distressed to think that she had heard of the affair of the horse, and more so to surmise that the gossip which clung to it must also have reached her. But I fear I thought most of her anxiety concerning me, which reflection caused my hand to shake from very happiness. "Y'r Flowers are beside me," and, "I beg you not Riske y'r Life Foolishly," and "I shall be very Miserable Indeed" But then: "Y'r Old Plamate & Well Wisher"! Nay, she was inscrutable as ever.

And my reply,—what was that to be? How I composed it in the state of mind I was in, I have no conception to this day. The chimney was clogged with papers ere (in a spelling to vie with Dolly's) I had set down my devotion, my undying devotion, to her interests. I asked forgiveness for my cruelty on that memorable morning I had last seen her. But even to allude to the bet with Chartersea was beyond my powers; and as for renouncing it, though for her sake,—that was not to be thought of. The high play I readily promised to avoid in the future, and I signed myself,—well, it matters not after seventy years.

The same day, Tuesday, I received a letter from his Grace of Chartersea saying that he looked to reach London that night, but very late. He begged that Mr. Fox and Lord Comyn and I would sup with him at the Star and Garter at eleven, to fix matters for the trial on the morrow. Mr. Fox could not go, but Comyn and I went to the inn, having first attended "The Tempest" at Drury Lane with Lady Di and Mr. Beauclerk.

We found his Grace awaiting us in a private room, with Captain Lewis, of the 60th Foot, who had figured as a second in the duel with young Atwater. The captain was a rake and a bully and a toadeater, of course, with a loud and profane tongue, and he had had a bottle too many in the duke's travelling-coach. There was likewise a Sir John Brooke, a country neighbour of his Grace in Nottinghamshire. Sir John apparently had no business in such company. He was a hearty, fox-hunting squire who had seen little of London; a three-bottle man who told a foul story and went asleep immediately afterwards. Much to my disappointment, Mr. Manners had gone to Arlington Street direct. I had longed for a chance to speak a little of my mind to him.

This meeting, which I shall not take the time to recount, was near to ending in an open breach of negotiations. His Grace had lost money at York, and more to Lewis on the way to London. He was in one of his vicious humours. He insisted that Hyde Park should be the place of the contest. In vain did Comyn and I plead for some less public spot on account of the disagreeable advertisement the matter had received. His Grace would be damned before he would yield; and Lewis, adding a more forcible contingency, hinted that our side feared a public trial. Comyn presently shut him up.

"Do you ride the horse after his Grace is thrown," says he, "and I agree to get on after and he does not kill you. 'Sdeath! I am not of the army," adds my Lord, cuttingly; "I am a seaman, and not supposed to know a stirrup from a snaffle."

"'Od's blood!" yelled the captain, "you question my horsemanship, my
Lord? Do I understand your Lordship to question my courage?"

"After I am thrown!" cries his Grace, very ugly, and fingering the jewels on his hilt.

Sir John was awakened by the noise, and turning heavily spilled the whole of a pint of port on the duke's satin waist coat and breeches. Whereat Chartersea in a rage flung the bottle at his head with a curse, which it seems was a habit with his Grace. But the servants coming in, headed by my old friend the chamberlain, they quieted down. And it was presently agreed that the horse was to be at noon in the King's Old Road, or Rotten Row (as it was then beginning to be called), in Hyde Park.

I shall carry to the grave the memory of the next day. I was up betimes, and over to the White

Horse Cellar to see Pollux groomed, where I found a crowd about the opening into the stable court. "The young American!" called some one, and to my astonishment and no small annoyance I was greeted with a "Huzzay for you, sir!" "My groat's on your honour!"

This good-will was owing wholly to the duke's unpopularity with all classes. Inside, sporting gentlemen in hunting-frocks of red and green, and velvet visored caps, were shouldering favoured 'ostlers from the different noblemen's stables; and there was a liberal sprinkling of the characters who attended the cock mains in Drury Lane and at Newmarket. At the moment of my arrival the head 'ostler was rubbing down the stallion's flank.

"Here's ten pounds to ride him, Saunders!" called one of the hunting-frocks.

"Umph!" sniffed the 'ostler; "ride 'im is it, yere honour? Two hunner beast eno', an' a Portugal crown i' th' boot. Sooner take me chaunces o' Tyburn on 'Ounslow 'Eath. An' Miller waurna able to sit 'im, 'tis no for th' likes o' me to try. Th' bloody devil took th' shirt off Teddy's back this morn. I adwises th' young Buckskin t' order 's coffin." Just then he perceived me, and touched his cap, something abashed. "With submission, sir, y'r honour'll take an old man's adwise an' not go near 'im."

Pollux's appearance, indeed, was not calculated to reassure me. He looked ugly to exaggeration, his ears laid back and his nostrils as big as crowns, and his teeth bared time and time. Now and anon an impatient fling of his hoof would make the grooms start away from him. Since coming to the inn he had been walked a couple of miles each day, with two men with loaded whips to control him. I was being offered a deal of counsel, when big Mr. Astley came in from Lambeth, and silenced them all.

"These grooms, Mr. Carvel," he said to me, as we took a bottle in private inside, "these grooms are the very devil for superstition. And once a horse gets a bad name with them, good-by to him. Miller knew how to ride, of course, but like many another of them, was too damned over-confident. I warned him more than once for getting young horses into a fret, and I'm willing to lay a ten-pound note that he angered Pollux. 'Od's life! He is a vicious beast. So was his father, Culloden, before him. But here's luck to you, sir!" says Mr. Astley, tipping his glass; "having seen you ride, egad! I have put all the money I can afford in your favour."

Before I left him he had given me several valuable hints as to the manner of managing that kind of a horse: not to auger him with the spurs unless it became plain that he meant to kill me; to try persuasion first and force afterwards; and secondly, he taught me a little trick of twisting the bit which I have since found very useful.

Leaving the White Horse, I was followed into Piccadilly by the crowd, until I was forced to take refuge in a hackney chaise. The noise of the affair had got around town, and I was heartily sorry I had not taken the other and better method of trying conclusions with the duke, and slapped his face. I found Jack Comyn in Dover Street, and presently Mr. Fox came for us with his chestnuts in his chaise, Fitzpatrick with him. At Hyde Park Corner there was quite a jam of coaches, chaises, and cabriolets and beribboned phaetons, which made way for us, but kept us busy bowing as we passed among them. It seemed as if everybody of consequence that I had met in London was gathered there. One face I missed, and rejoiced that she was absent, for I had a degraded feeling like that of being the favourite in a cudgel-bout. And the thought that her name was connected with all this made my face twitch. I heard the people clapping and saw them waving in the carriages as we passed, and some stood forward before the rest in a haphazard way, without rhyme or reason. Mr. Walpole with Lady Di Beauclerk, and Mr. Storer and Mr. Price and Colonel St. John, and Lord and Lady Carlisle and Lady Ossory. These I recognized. Inside, the railing along the row was lined with people. And there stood Pollux, bridled, with a blanket thrown over his great back and chest, surrounded still by the hunting-frocks, who had followed him from the White Horse. Mixed in with these, swearing, conjecturing, and betting, were some to surprise me, whose names were connected with every track in England: the Duke of Grafton and my Lords Sandwich and March and Bolingbroke, and Sir Charles Bunbury, and young Lords Derby and Foley, who, after establishing separate names for folly on the tracks, went into partnership. My Lord Baltimore descended listlessly from his cabriolet to join the group. They all sang out when they caught sight of our party, and greeted me with a zeal to carry me off my feet. And my

Lord Sandwich, having done me the honour to lay something very handsome upon me, had his chief jockey on hand to give me some final advice. I believe I was the coolest of any of them. And at that time of all others the fact came up to me with irresistible humour that I, a young colonial Whig, who had grown up to detest these people, should be rubbing noses with them.

The duke put in an appearance five minutes before the hour, upon a bay gelding, and attended by Lewis and Sir John Brooke, both mounted. As a most particular evidence of the detestation in which Chartersea was held, he could find nothing in common with such notorious rakes as March and Sandwich. And it fell to me to champion these. After some discussion between Fox and Captain Lewis, March was chosen umpire. His Lordship took his post in the middle of the Row, drew forth an enamelled repeater from his waistcoat, and mouthed out the conditions of the match,—the terms, as he said, being private.

"Are you ready, Mr. Carvel?" he asked.

"I am, my Lord," I answered. The bells were pealing noon.

"Then mount, sir," said he.

The voices of the people dropped to a hum that brought to mind the long forgotten sound of the bees swarming in the garden by the Chesapeake. My breath began to come quickly. Through the sunny haze I saw the cows and deer grazing by the Serpentine, and out of the back of my eye handkerchiefs floated from the carriages banked at the gate. They took the blanket off the stallion.

Stall-fed, and excited by the crowd, he looked brutal indeed. The faithful Banks, in a new suit of the Carvel livery, held the stirrup, and whispered a husky "God keep you, sir!" Suddenly I was up. The murmur was hushed, and the Park became still as a peaceful farm in Devonshire. The grooms let go of the stallion's head.

He stood trembling like the throes of death. I gripped my knees as Captain Daniel had taught me, years ago, when some invisible force impelled me to look aside. From between the broad and hunching shoulders of Chartersea I met such a venomous stare as a cattle-fish might use to freeze his prey. Cattle—fish! The word kept running over my tongue. I thought of the snaky arms that had already caught Mr. Marmaduke, and were soon, perhaps, to entangle Dorothy. She had begged me not to ride, and I was risking a life which might save hers.

The wind rushing in my ears and beating against my face awoke me all at once. The trees ran madly past, and the water at my right was a silver blur. The beast beneath me snorted as he rose and fell. Fainter and fainter dropped the clamour behind me, which had risen as I started, and the leaps grew longer and longer. Then my head was cleared like a steamed window-pane in a cold blast. I saw the road curve in front of me, I put all my strength into the curb, and heeling at a fearful angle was swept into the busy Kensington Road. For the first time I knew what it was to fear a horse. The stallion's neck was stretched, his shoes rang on the cobbles, and my eyes were fixed on a narrow space between carriages coming together. In a flash I understood why the duke had insisted upon Hyde Park, and that nerved me some. I saw the frightened coachmen pulling their horses this way and that, I heard the cries of the foot-passengers, and then I was through, I know not how. Once more I summoned all my power, recalled the twist Astley had spoken of, and tried it. I bent his neck for an inch of rein. Next I got another inch, and then came a taste—the smallest taste—of mastery like elixir. The motion changed with it, became rougher, and the hoof-beats a fraction less frequent. He steered like a ship with sail reduced. In and out we dodged among the wagons, and I was beginning to think I had him, when suddenly, without a move of warning, he came down rigid with his feet planted together, and only a miracle and my tight grip restrained me from shooting over his head. There he stood shaking and snorting, nor any persuasion would move him. I resorted at last to the spurs.

He was up in the air in an instant, and came down across the road. Again I dug in to the rowels, and clung the tighter, and this time he landed with his head to London. A little knot of people had collected to watch me, and out stepped a strapping fellow in the King's scarlet, from the Guard's Horse near by.

"Hold him, sir!" he said, tipping. "Better dismount, sir. He means murder, y'r honour."

"Keep clear, curse you!" I cried, waving him off. "What time is it?"

He stepped back, no doubt thinking me mad. Some one spoke up and said it was five minutes past noon. I had the grace to thank him, I believe.

To my astonishment I had been gone but four minutes; they had seemed twenty. Looking about me, I found I was in the open space before old Kensington Church, over against the archway there. Once more I dug in the spurs, this time with success. Almost at a jump the beast took me into the angle of posts to the east of the churchyard gate and tore up the footpath of Church Lane, terrified men and women ahead of me taking to the kennel. He ran irregularly, now on the side of the posts, now against the bricks, and then I gave myself up.

Heaven put a last expedient into my head, that I had once heard Mr. Dulany speak of. I braced myself for a pull that should have broken the stallion's jaw and released his mouth altogether. Incredible as it may seem, he jarred into a trot, and presently came down to a walk, tossing his head like fury, and sweating at every pore. I leaned over and patted him, speaking him fair, and (marvel of marvels!) when we had got to the dogs that guard the entrance of Camden House I had coaxed him around and into the street, and cantered back at easy speed to the church. Without pausing to speak to the bunch that stood at the throat of the lane, I started toward London, thankfulness and relief swelling within me. I understood the beast, and spoke to him when he danced aside at a wagon with bells or a rattling load of coals, and checked him with a word and a light hand.

Before I gained the Life Guard's House I met a dozen horsemen, amongst them Banks on a mount of Mr. Fox's. They shouted when they saw me, Colonel St. John calling out that he had won another hundred that I was not dead. Sir John Brooke puffed and swore he did not begrudge his losses to see me safe, despite Captain Lewis's sourness. Storey vowed he would give a dinner in my honour, and, riding up beside me, whispered that he was damned sorry the horse was now broken, and his Grace's chance of being killed taken away. And thus escorted, I came in by the King's New Road to avoid the people running in the Row, and so down to Hyde Park Corner, and in among the chaises and the phaetons, where there was enough cheering and waving of hats and handkerchiefs to please the most exacting of successful generals. I rode up to my Lord March, and finding there was a minute yet to run I went up the Row a distance and back again amidst more huzzaing, Pollux prancing and quivering, and frothing his bit, but never once attempting to break.

When I had got down, they pressed around me until I could scarce breathe, crying congratulations, Comyn embracing me openly. Mr. Fox vowed he had never seen so fine a sight, and said many impolitic things which the duke must have overheard . . . . Lady Carlisle sent me a red rose for my buttonhole by his Lordship. Mr. Warner, the lively parson with my Lord March, desired to press my hand, declaring that he had won a dozen of port upon me, which he had set his best cassock against. My Lord Sandwich offered me snuff, and invited me to Hichinbroke. Indeed, I should never be through were I to continue. But I must not forget my old acquaintance Mr. Walpole, who protested that he must get permission to present me to Princess Amelia: that her Royal Highness would not rest content now, until she had seen me. I did not then know her Highness's sporting propensity.

Then my Lord March called upon the duke, who stood in the midst of an army of his toadeaters. I almost pitied him then, tho' I could not account for the feeling. I think it was because a nobleman with so great a title should be so cordially hated and despised. There were high words along the railing among the duke's supporters, Captain Lewis, in his anger, going above an inference that the stallion had been broken privately. Chartersea came forward with an indifferent swagger, as if to say as much: and, in truth, no one looked for more sport, and some were even turning away. He had scarce put foot to the stirrup, when the surprise came. Two minutes were up before he was got in the saddle, Pollux rearing and plunging and dancing in a circle, the grooms shouting and dodging, and his Grace cursing in a voice to wake the dead and Mr. Fox laughing, and making small wagers that he would never be mounted. But at last the duke was up and gripped, his face bloody red, giving vent to his fury with the spurs.

Then something happened, and so quickly that it cannot be writ fast enough. Pollux bolted like a shot out of a sling, vaulted the railing as easily as you or I would hop over a stick, and galloping across the lawn and down the embankment flung his Grace into the Serpentine. Precisely, as Mr. Fox afterwards remarked, as the swine with the evil spirits ran down the slope into the sea.

An indescribable bedlam of confusion followed, lords and gentlemen, tradesmen and grooms, hostlers and apprentices, all tumbling after, many crying with laughter. My Lord Sandwich's jockey pulled his Grace from the water in a most pitiable state of rage and humiliation. His side curls gone, the powder and pomatum washed from his hair, bedraggled and muddy and sputtering oaths, he made his way to Lord March, swearing by all divine that a trick was put on him, that he would ride the stallion to Land's End. His Lordship, pulling his face straight, gravely informed the duke that the match was over. With this his Grace fell flatly sullen, was pushed into a coach by Sir John and the captain, and drove rapidly off Kensington way, to avoid the people at the corner.

CHAPTER XXXVIII

IN WHICH I AM ROUNDLY BROUGHT TO TASK

I would have gone to Arlington Street direct, but my friends had no notion of letting me escape. They carried me off to Brooks's Club, where a bowl of punch was brewed directly, and my health was drunk to three times three. Mr. Storer commanded a turtle dinner in my honour. We were not many, fortunately,—only Mr. Fox's little coterie. And it was none other than Mr. Fox who made the speech of the evening. "May I be strung as high as Haman," said he, amid a tempest of laughter, "if ever I saw half so edifying a sight as his Grace pitching into the Serpentine, unless it were his Grace dragged out again. Mr. Carvel's advent has been a Godsend to us narrow ignoramuses of this island, gentlemen. To the Englishmen of our colonies, sirs, and that we may never underrate or misunderstand them more!"

"Nay, Charles," cried my Lord Comyn. "Where is our gallantry? I give you first the Englishwomen of our colonies, and in particular the pride of Maryland, who has brought back to the old country all the graces of the new,—Miss Manners."

His voice was drowned by a deafening shout, and we charged our glasses to drain them brimming. And then we all went to Drury Lane to see Mrs. Clive romp through 'The Wonder' in the spirit of the "immortal Peg." She spoke an epilogue that Mr. Walpole had writ especial for her, and made some witty and sarcastic remarks directed at the gentlemen in our stagebox. We topped off a very full day by a supper at the Bedford Arms, where I must draw the certain.

The next morning I was abed at an hour which the sobriety of old age makes me blush abed think of. Banks had just concluded a discreet discourse upon my accomplishment of the day before, and had left for my newspapers, when he came running back with the information that Miss Manners would see my honour that day. There was no note. Between us we made my toilet in a jiffy, and presently I was walking in at the Manners's door in an amazing hurry, and scarcely waited for a direction. But as I ran up the stairs, I heard the tinkle of the spinet, and the notes of an old, familiar tune fell upon my ears. The words rose in my head with the cadence.

"Love me little, love me long,
Is the burthen of my song,
Love that is too hot and strong
Runneth soon to waste."

That simple air, already mellowed by an hundred years, had always been her favourite. She used to sing it softly to herself as we roamed the woods and fields of the Eastern Shore. Instinctively I paused at the dressing-room door. Nay, my dears, you need not cry out, such was the custom of the times. A dainty bower it was, filled with the perfume of flowers, and rosy cupids disporting on the ceiling; and china and silver and gold filigree strewn about, with my tea-cups on the table. The sunlight fell like a halo round Dorothy's head, her hands strayed over the keys, and her eyes were far away. She had not heard me. I remember her dress,—a silk with blue cornflowers on a light ground, and the flimsiest of lace caps resting on her hair. I thought her face paler; but beyond that she did not show her illness.

She looked up, and perceived me, I thought, with a start. "So it is you!" she said demurely enough; "you are come at last to give an account of yourself."

"Are you better, Dorothy?" I asked earnestly.

"Why should you think that I have been ill?" she replied, her fingers going back to the spinet. "It is a mistake, sir. Dr. James has given me near a gross of his infamous powders, and is now exploiting another cure. I have been resting from the fatigues of London, while you have been wearing yourself out."

"Dr. James himself told me your condition was serious," I said.

"Of course," said she; "the worse the disease, the more remarkable the cure, the more sought after the physician. When will you get over your provincial simplicity?"

I saw there was nothing to be got out of her while in this baffling humour. I wondered what devil impelled a woman to write one way and talk another. In her note to me she had confessed her illness. The words I had formed to say to her were tied on my tongue. But on the whole I congratulated myself. She knew how to step better than I, and there were many awkward things between us of late best not spoken of. But she kept me standing an unconscionable time without a word, which on the whole was cruelty, while she played over some of Dibdin's ballads.

"Are you in a hurry, sir," she asked at length, turning on me with a smile, "are you in a hurry to join my Lord March or his Grace of Grafton? And have you writ Captain Clapsaddle and your Whig friends at home of your new intimacies, of Mr. Fox and my Lord Sandwich?"

I was dumb.

"Yes, you must be wishing to get away," she continued cruelly, picking up the newspaper. "I had forgotten this notice. When I saw it this morning I thought of you, and despaired of a glimpse of you to-day." (Reading.) "At the Three Hats, Islington, this day, the 10th of May, will be played a grand match at that ancient and much renowned manly diversion called Double Stick by a sect of chosen young men at that exercise from different parts of the West Country, for two guineas given free; those who break the most heads to bear away the prize. Before the above-mentioned diversion begins, Mr. Sampson and his young German will display alternately on one, two, and three horses, various surprising and curious feats of famous horsemanship in like manner as at the Grand Jubilee at Stratford-upon-Avon. Admittance one shilling each person.' Before you leave, Mr. Richard," she continued, with her eyes still on the sheet, "I should like to talk over one or two little matters."

"Dolly—!"

"Will you sit, sir?"

I sat down uneasily, expecting the worst. She disappointed me, as usual.

"What an unspeakable place must you keep in Dover Street! I cannot send even a footman there but what he comes back reeling."

I had to laugh at this. But there was no smile out of my lady.

"It took me near an hour and a half to answer your note," I replied.

"And 'twas a masterpiece!" exclaimed Dolly, with withering sarcasm; "oh, a most amazing masterpiece, I'll be bound! His worship the French Ambassador is a kitten at diplomacy beside you, sir. An hour and a half, did you say, sir? Gemini, the Secretary of State and his whole corps could not have composed the like in a day."

"Faith!" I cried, with feeling enough; "and if that is diplomacy, I would rather make leather breeches than be given an embassy."

She fixed her eyes upon me so disconcertingly that mine fell.

"There was a time," she said, with a change of tone, "there was a time when a request of mine, and it were not granted outright, would have received some attention. This is my first experience at being ignored."

"I had made a wager," said I, "and could not retract with honour."

"So you had made a wager! Now we are to have some news at last. How stupid of you, Richard, not to tell me before. I confess I wonder what these wits find in your company. Here am I who have seen naught but dull women for a fortnight, and you have failed to say anything amusing in a quarter of an hour. Let us hear about the wager."

"Where is little to tell," I answered shortly, considerably piqued.
"I bet your friend, the Duke of Chartersea, some hundreds of pounds I
could ride Lord Baltimore's Pollux for twenty minutes, after which his

Grace was to get on and ride twenty more."

"Where did you see the duke?" Dolly interrupted, without much show of interest.

I explained how we had met him at Brooks's, and had gone to his house.

"You went to his house?" she repeated, raising her eyebrows a trifle; "and Comyn and Mr. Fox? And pray, how did this pretty subject come up?"

I related, very badly, I fear, Fox's story of young Wrottlesey and the tea-merchant's daughter. And what does my lady do but get up and turn her back, arranging some pinks in the window. I could have sworn she was laughing, had I not known better.

"Well?"

"Well, that was a reference to a little pleasantry Mr. Fox had put up on him some time before. His Grace flared, but tried not to show it. He said he had heard I could do something with a horse (I believe he made it up), and Comyn gave oath that I could; and then he offered to bet Comyn that I could not ride this Pollux, who had killed his groom. That made me angry, and I told the duke I was no jockey to be put up to decide wagers, and that he must make his offers to me."

"La!" said Dolly, "you fell in head over heels."

"What do you mean by that?" I demanded.

"Nothing," said she, biting her lip. "Come, you are as ponderous as Dr. Johnson."

"Then Mr. Fox proposed that his Grace should ride after me."

Here Dolly laughed in her handkerchief.

"I'll be bound," said she.

"Then the duke went to York," I continued hurriedly; and when he came back we met him at the Star and Garter. He insisted that the match should come off in Hyde Park. I should have preferred the open roads north of Bedford House."

"Where there is no Serpentine," she interrupted, with the faintest suspicion of a twinkle about her eyes. "On, sir, on! You are as reluctant as our pump at Wilmot House in the dry season. I see you were not killed, as you richly deserved. Let us have the rest of your tale."

"There is very little more to it, save that I contrived to master the beast, and his Grace—"

"—Was disgraced. A vastly fine achievement, surely. But where are you to stop? You will be shaming the King next by outwalking him. Pray, how did the duke appear as he was going into the Serpentine?"

"You have heard?" I exclaimed, the trick she had played me dawning upon me.

"Upon my word, Richard, you are more of a simpleton than I thought you.
Have you not seen your newspaper this morning?"

I explained how it was that I had not. She took up the Chronicle.

"'This Mr. Carvel has made no inconsiderable noise since his arrival in town, and yesterday crowned his performances by defeating publicly a noble duke at a riding match in Hyde Park, before half the quality of the kingdom. His Lordship of March and Ruglen acted as umpire.' There, sir, was I not right to beg Sir John Fielding to put you in safe keeping until your grandfather can send for you?"

I made to seize the paper, but she held it from me.

"'If Mr. Carvel remains long enough in England, he bids fair to share the talk of Mayfair with a certain honourable young gentleman of Brooks's and the Admiralty, whose debts and doings now furnish most of the gossip for the clubs and the card tables. Their names are both connected with this contest. 'Tis whispered that the wager upon which the match was ridden arose—'" here Dolly stopped shortly, her colour mounting, and cried out with a stamp of her foot. "You are not content to bring publicity upon yourself, who deserve it, but must needs drag innocent names into the newspapers."

"What have they said?" I demanded, ready to roll every printer in London in the kennel.

"Nay, you may read for yourself," said she. And, flinging the paper in my lap, left the room.

They had not said much more, Heaven be praised. But I was angry and mortified as I had never been before, realizing for the first time what a botch I had made of my stay in London. In great dejection, I was picking up my hat to leave the house, when Mrs. Manners came in upon me, and insisted that I should stay for dinner. She was very white, and seemed troubled and preoccupied, and said that Mr. Manners had come back from York with a cold on his chest, but would insist upon joining the party to Vauxhall on Monday. I asked her when she was going to the baths, and suggested that the change would do her good. Indeed, she looked badly.

"We are not going, Richard," she replied; "Dorothy will not hear of it.
In spite of the doctor she says she is not ill, and must attend at
Vauxhall, too. You are asked?"

I said that Mr. Storer had included me. I am sure, from the way she looked at me, that she did not heed my answer. She appeared to hesitate on the verge of a speech, and glanced once or twice at the doors.

"Richard, I suppose you are old enough to take care of yourself, tho' you seem still a child to me. I pray you will be careful, my boy," she said, with something of the affection she had always borne me, "for your grandfather's sake, I pray you will run into no more danger. I—we are your old friends, and the only ones here to advise you."

She stopped, seemingly, to weigh the wisdom of what was to come next, while I leaned forward with an eagerness I could not hide. Was she to speak of the Duke of Chartersea? Alas, I was not to know. For at that moment Dorothy came back to inquire why I was not gone to the cudgelling at the Three Hats. I said I had been invited to stay to dinner.

"Why, I have writ a note asking Comyn," said she. "Do you think the house will hold you both?"

His Lordship came in as we were sitting down, bursting with some news, and he could hardly wait to congratulate Dolly on her recovery before he delivered it.

"Why, Richard," says the dog, "what do you think some wag has done now?
They believe at Brooks's 'twas that jackanapes of a parson, Dr. Warner,
who was there yesterday with March." He drew a clipping from his pocket.
"Listen, Miss Dolly:

"On Wednesday did a carter see
His Grace, the Duke of Ch-rt—s-a,
As plump and helpless as a bag,
A-straddle of a big-boned nag.
"Lord, Sam!" the carter loudly yelled,
On by this wondrous sight impelled,
"We'll run and watch this noble gander
Master a steed, like Alexander."
But, when the carter reached the Row,
His Grace had left it, long ago.
Bucephalus had leaped the green,
The duke was in the Serpentine.
The fervent wish of all good men
That he may ne'er come out again!'"

Comyn's impudence took my breath, tho' the experiment interested me not a little. My lady was pleased to laugh at the doggerel, and even Mrs. Manners. Its effect upon Mr. Marmaduke was not so spontaneous. His smile was half-hearted. Indeed, the little gentleman seemed to have lost his spirits, and said so little (for him), that I was encouraged to corner him that very evening and force him to a confession. But I might have known he was not to be caught. It appeared almost as if he guessed my purpose, for as soon as ever the claret was come on, he excused himself, saying he was promised to Lady

Harrington, who wanted one.

Comyn and I departed early on account of Dorothy. She had denied a dozen who had left cards upon her.

"Egad, Richard," said my Lord, when we had got to my lodgings, "I made him change colour, did I not? Do you know how the little fool looks to me? 'Od's life, he looks hunted, and cursed near brought to earth. We must fetch this thing to a point, Richard. And I am wondering what Chartersea's next move will be," he added thoughtfully.

CHAPTER XXXIX

HOLLAND HOUSE

On the morrow, as I was setting out to dine at Brooks's, I received the following on a torn slip of paper: "Dear Richard, we shall have a good show to-day you may care to see." It was signed "Fox," and dated at St. Stephen's. I lost no time in riding to Westminster, where I found a flock of excited people in Parliament Street and in the Palace Yard.

And on climbing the wide stone steps outside and a narrower flight within I was admitted directly into the august presence of the representatives of the English people. They were in a most prodigious and unseemly state of uproar.

What a place is old St. Stephen's Chapel, over St. Mary's in the Vaults, for the great Commons of England to gather! It is scarce larger or more imposing than our own assembly room in the Stadt House in Annapolis. St. Stephen's measures but ten yards by thirty, with a narrow gallery running along each side for visitors. In one of these, by the rail, I sat down suffocated, bewildered, and deafened. And my first impression out of the confusion was of the bewigged speaker enthroned under the royal arms, sore put to restore order. On the table in front of him lay the great mace of the Restoration. Three chandeliers threw down their light upon the mob of honourable members, and I wondered what had put them into this state of uproar.

Presently, with the help of a kind stranger on my right, who was occasionally making shorthand notes, I got a few bearings. That was the Treasury Bench, where Lord North sat (he was wide awake, now). And there was the Government side. He pointed out Barrington and Weymouth and Jerry Dyson and Sandwich, and Rigby in the court suit of purple velvet with the sword thrust through the pocket. I took them all in, as some of the worst enemies my country had in Britain. Then my informant seemed to hesitate, and made bold to ask my persuasion. When I told him I was a Whig, and an American, he begged the favour of my hand.

"There, sir," he cried excitedly, "that stout young gentleman with the black face and eyebrows, and the blacker heart, I may say,—the one dressed in the fantastical costume called by a French name, —is Mr. Charles Fox. He has been sent by the devil himself, I believe, to ruin this country. 'Ods, sir, that devil Lord Holland begot him. He is but one and twenty, but his detestable arts have saved North's neck from Burke and Wedderburn on two occasions this year."

"And what has happened to-day?" I asked, smiling.

The stranger smiled, too.

"Why, sir," he answered, raising his voice above the noise; "if you have been in London any length of time, you will have read the account, with comment, of the Duke of Grafton's speech in the Lords, signed Domitian. Their Lordships well know it should have been over a greater signature. This afternoon his Grace of Manchester was talking in the Upper House about the Spanish troubles, when Lord Gower arose and desired that the place might be cleared of strangers, lest some Castilian spy might lurk under the gallery. That was directed against us of the press, sir, and their Lordships knew it. 'Ad's heart, sir, there was a riot, the house servants tumbling everybody out, and Mr. Burke and Mr. Dunning in the boot, who were gone there on the business of this house to present a bill. Those gentlemen are but just back, calling upon the commons to revenge them and vindicate their honour. And my Lord North looks troubled, as you will mark, for the matter is like to go hard against his Majesty's friends. But hush, Mr. Burke is to speak."

The horse fell quiet to listen, and my friend began to ply his shorthand industriously. I leaned forward with a sharp curiosity to see this great friend of America. He was dressed in a well-worn suit of brown, and I recall a decided Irish face, and a more decided Irish accent, which presently I forgot under the spell of his eloquence. I have heard it said he had many defects of delivery. He had none that day, or else I was too little experienced to note them. Afire with indignation, he told how the deputy black rod had hustled him like a vagabond or a thief, and he called the House of Lords a bear garden. He was followed by Dunning, in a still more inflammatory mood, until it seemed as if all the King's friends in the Lower House must desert their confederates in the Upper. No less important a retainer than Mr. Onslow moved a policy of retaliation, and those that were left began to act like the Egyptians when they felt the Red Sea under them. They nodded and whispered in their consternation.

It was then that Mr. Fox got calmly up before the pack of frightened mercenaries and argued (God save the mark!) for moderation. He had the ear of the house in a second, and he spoke with all the confidence—this youngster who had just reached his majority—he had used with me before his intimates. I gaped with astonishment and admiration. The Lords, said he, had plainly meant no insult to this honourable house, nor yet to the honourable members. They had aimed at the common enemies of man, the printers. And for this their heat was more than pardonable. My friend at my side stopped his writing to swear under his breath. "Look at 'em!" he cried; "they are turning already. He could argue Swedenborg into popery!"

The deserters were coming back to the ranks, indeed, and North and Dyson and Weymouth had ceased to look haggard, and were wreathed in smiles. In vain did Mr. Burke harangue them in polished phrase. It was a language North and Company did not understand, and cared not to learn. Their young champion spoke the more worldly and cynical tongue of White's and Brooks's, with its shorter sentences and absence of formality. And even as the devil can quote Scripture to his purpose, Mr. Fox quoted history and the classics, with plenty more that was not above the heads of the booted and spurred country squires. And thus, for the third time, he earned the gratitude of his gracious Majesty.

"Well, Richard," said he, slipping his arm through mine as we came out into Parliament Street, "I promised you some sport. Have you enjoyed it?"

I was forced to admit that I had.

"Let us to the 'Thatched House,' and have supper privately," he suggested. "I do not feel like a company to-night." We walked on for some time in silence. Presently he said:

"You must not leave us, Richard. You may go home to see your grandfather die, and when you come back I will see about getting you a little borough for what my father paid for mine. And you shall marry Dorothy, and perchance return in ten years as governor of a principality. That is, after we've ruined you at the club. How does that prospect sit?"

I wondered at the mood he was in, that made him choose me rather than the adulation and applause he was sure to receive at Brooks's for the part he had played that night. After we had satisfied our hunger,—for neither of us had dined,—and poured out a bottle of claret, he looked up at me quizzically.

"I have not heard you congratulate me," he said.

"Nor will you," I replied, laughing.

"I like you the better for it, Richard. 'Twas a damned poor performance, and that's truth."

"I thought the performance remarkable," I said honestly.

"Oh, but it was not," he answered scornfully. "The moment that dun-coloured Irishman gets up, the whole government pack begins to whine and shiver. There are men I went to school with I fear more than Burke. But you don't like to see the champion of America come off second best. Is that what you're thinking?"

"No. But I was wondering why you have devoted your talents to the devil," I said, amazed at my boldness.

He glanced at me, and half laughed again.

"You are cursed frank," said he; "damned frank."

"But you invited it."

"Yes," he replied, "so I did. Give me a man who is honest. Fill up again," said he; "and spit out all you would like to say, Richard."

"Then," said I, "why do you waste your time and your breath in defending a crew of political brigands and placemen, and a king who knows not the meaning of the word gratitude, and who has no use for a man of ability? You have honoured me with your friendship, Charles Fox, and I may take the liberty to add that you seem to love power more than spoils. You have originality. You are honest enough to think and act upon your own impulses. And pardon me if I say you have very little chance on that side of the house where you have put yourself."

"You seem to have picked up a trifle since you came into England," he said. "A damned shrewd estimate, I'll be sworn. And for a colonial! But, as for power," he added a little doggedly, "I have it in plenty, and the kind I like. The King and North hate and fear me already more than Wilkes."

"And with more cause," I replied warmly. "His Majesty perhaps knows that you understand him better, and foresees the time when a man of your character will give him cause to fear indeed."

He did not answer that, but called for a reckoning; and taking my arm again, we walked out past the sleeping houses.

"Have you ever thought much of the men we have in the colonies?" I asked.

"No," he replied; "Chatham stands for 'em, and I hate Chatham on my father's account. That is reason enough for me."

"You should come back to America with me," I said. "And when you had rested awhile at Carvel

Hall, I would ride with you through the length of the provinces from Massachusetts to North Carolina. You will see little besides hard-working, self-respecting Englishmen, loyal to a king who deserves loyalty as little as Louis of France. But with their eyes open, and despite the course he has taken. They are men whose measure of resolution is not guessed at."

He was silent again until we had got into Piccadilly and opposite his lodgings.

"Are they all like you?" he demanded.

"Who?" said I. For I had forgotten my words.

"The Americans."

"The greater part feel as I do."

"I suppose you are for bed," he remarked abruptly.

"The night is not yet begun," I answered, repeating his favourite words, and pointing at the glint of the sun on the windows.

"What do you say to a drive behind those chestnuts of mine, for a breath of air? I have just got my new cabriolet Selwyn ordered in Paris."

Soon we were rattling over the stones in Piccadilly, wrapped in greatcoats, for the morning wind was cold. We saw the Earl of March and Ruglen getting out of a chair before his house, opposite the Green Park, and he stopped swearing at the chairmen to wave at us.

"Hello, March!" Mr. Fox said affably, "you're drunk."

His Lordship smiled, bowed graciously if unsteadily to me, and did not appear to resent the pleasantry. Then he sighed.

"What a pair of cubs it is," said he; "I wish to God I was young again.

I hear you astonished the world again last night, Charles."

We left him being assisted into his residence by a sleepy footman, paid our toll at Hyde Park Corner, and rolled onward toward Kensington, Fox laughing as we passed the empty park at the thought of what had so lately occurred there. After the close night of St. Stephen's, nature seemed doubly beautiful. The sun slanted over the water in the gardens in bars of green and gold. The bright new leaves were on the trees, and the morning dew had brought with it the smell of the living earth. We passed the stream of market wagons lumbering along, pulled by sturdy, patient farm-horses, driven by smocked countrymen, who touched their caps to the fine gentlemen of the court end of town; who shook their heads and exchanged deep tones over the whims of quality, unaccountable as the weather. But one big-chested fellow arrested his salute, a scowl came over his face, and he shouted back to the wagoner whose horses were munching his hay:

"Hi, Jeems, keep down yere hands. Mr. Fox is noo friend of we."

This brought a hard smile on Mr. Fox's face.

"I believe, Richard," he said, "I have become more detested than any man in Parliament."

"And justly," I replied; "for you have fought all that is good in you."

"I was mobbed once, in Parliament Street. I thought they would kill me.

Have you ever been mobbed, Richard?" he asked

indifferently.

"Never, I thank Heaven," I answered fervently.

"I think I would rather be mobbed than indulge in any amusement I know of," he continued. "Than confound Wedderburn, or drive a measure against Burke,—which is no bad sport, my word on't. I would rather be mobbed than have my horse win at Newmarket. There is a keen pleasure you wot not of, my lad, in listening to Billingsgate and Spitalfields howl maledictions upon you. And no sensation I know of is equal to that of the moment when the mud and sticks and oranges are coming through the windows of your coach, when the dirty weavers are clutching at your ruffles and shaking their filthy fists under your nose."

"It is, at any rate, strictly an aristocratic pleasure," I assented, laughing.

So we came to Holland House. Its wide fields of sprouting corn, its woods and pastures and orchards in blossom, were smiling that morning, as though Leviathan, the town, were not rolling onward to swallow them. Lord Holland had bought the place from the Warwicks, with all its associations and memories. The capped towers and quaint facades and projecting windows were plain to be seen from where we halted in the shaded park, and to the south was that Kensington Road we had left, over which all the glory and royalty of England at one time or another had rolled. Under these majestic oaks and cedars Cromwell and Ireton had stood while the beaten Royalists lashed their horses on to Brentford. Nor did I forget that the renowned Addison had lived here after his unhappy marriage with Lady Warwick, and had often ridden hence to Button's Coffee House in town, where my grandfather had had his dinner with Dean Swift.

We sat gazing at the building, which was bathed in the early sun, at the deer and sheep grazing in the park, at the changing colours of the young leaves as the breeze swayed them. The market wagons had almost ceased now, and there was little to break the stillness.

"You love the place?" I said.

He started, as though I had awakened him out of a sleep. And he was no longer the Fox of the clubs, the cynical, the reckless. He was no longer the best-dressed man in St. James's Street, or the aggressive youngster of St. Stephen's.

"Love it!" he cried. "Ay, Richard, and few guess how well. You will not laugh when I tell you that my happiest days have been passed here, when I was but a chit, in the long room where Addison used to walk up and down composing his Spectators: or trotting after my father through these woods and gardens. A kinder parent does not breathe than he. Well I remember how he tossed me in his arms under that tree when I had thrashed another lad for speaking ill of him. He called me his knight. In all my life he has never broken faith with me. When they were blasting down a wall where those palings now stand, he promised me I should see it done, and had it rebuilt and blown down again because I had missed the sight. All he ever exacted of me was that I should treat him as an elder brother. He had his own notion of the world I was going into, and prepared me accordingly. He took me from Eton to Spa, where I learned gaming instead of Greek, and gave me so much a night to risk at play."

I looked at him in astonishment. To say that I thought these relations strange would have been a waste of words.

"To be sure," Charles continued, "I was bound to learn, and could acquire no younger." He flicked the glossy red backs of his horses with his whip. "You are thinking it an extraordinary education, I know," he added rather sadly. "I hav a-told you this —God knows why! Yes, because I like you damnably, and you would have heard worse elsewhere, both of him and of me. I fear you have listened to the world's opinion of Lord Holland."

Indeed, I had heard a deal of that nobleman's peculations of the public funds. But in this he was no worse than the bulk of his colleagues. His desertion of William Pitt I found hard to forgive.

"The best father in the world, Richard!" cried Charles. "If his former friends could but look into his kind heart, and see him in his home, they would not have turned their backs upon him. I do not mean such scoundrels as Rigby. And now my father is in exile half the year in Nice, and the other half at King's Gate. The King and Jack Bute used him for a tool, and then cast him out. You wonder why I am of the King's party?" said he, with something sinister in his smile; "I will tell you. When I got my borough I cared not a fig for parties or principles. I had only the one definite ambition, to revenge Lord Holland. Nay," he exclaimed, stopping my protest, "I was not too young to know rottenness as well as another. The times are rotten in England. You may have virtue in America, amongst a people which is fresh from a struggle with the earth and its savages. We have cursed little at home, in faith. The King, with his barley water and rising at six, and shivering in chapel, and his middle-class table, is rottener than the rest. The money he saves in his damned beggarly court goes to buy men's souls. His word is good with none. For my part I prefer a man who is drunk six days out of the seven to one who takes his pleasure so. And I am not so great a fool that I cannot distinguish justice from injustice. I know the wrongs of the colonies, which you yourself have put as clear as I wish to hear, despite Mr. Burke and his eloquence.

[My grandfather has made a note here, which in justice should be

added, that he was not deceived by Mr. Fox's partiality.—D. C. C.]

And perhaps, Richard," he concluded, with a last lingering look at the old pile as he turned his horses, "perhaps some day, I shall remember what you told us at Brooks's."

It was thus, boyishly, that Mr. Fox chose to take me into his confidence, an honour which I shall remember with a thrill to my dying day. So did he reveal to me the impulses of his early life, hidden forever from his detractors. How little does the censure of this world count, which cannot see the heart behind the embroidered waistcoat! When

Charles Fox began his career he was a thoughtless lad, but steadfast to such principles as he had formed for himself. They were not many, but, compared to those of the arena which he entered, they were noble. He strove to serve his friends, to lift the name of a father from whom he had received nothing but kindness, however misguided. And when he saw at length the error of his ways, what a mighty blow did he strike for the right!

"Here is a man," said Dr. Johnson, many years afterwards, "who has divided his kingdom with Caesar; so that it was a doubt whether the nation should be ruled by the sceptre of George the Third or the tongue of Fox."

CHAPTER XL

VAUXHALL

Matters had come to a pretty pickle indeed. I was openly warned at Brooks's and elsewhere to beware of the duke, who was said upon various authority to be sulking in Hanover Square, his rage all the more dangerous because it was smouldering. I saw Dolly only casually before the party to Vauxhall. Needless to say, she flew in the face of Dr. James's authority, and went everywhere. She was at Lady Bunbury's drum, whither I had gone in another fruitless chase after Mr. Marmaduke. Dr. Warner's verse was the laughter of the company. And, greatly to my annoyance,—in the circumstances,—I was made a hero of, and showered with three times as many invitations as I could accept.

The whole story got abroad, even to the awakening of the duke in Covent Garden. And that clownish Mr. Foote, of the Haymarket, had added some lines to a silly popular song entitled 'The Sights o' Lunnun', with which I was hailed at Mrs. Betty's fruit-stall in St. James's Street. Here is one of the verses:

"In Maryland, he hunts the Fox
From dewy Morn till Day grows dim;
At Home he finds a Paradox,
From Noon till Dawn the Fox hunts him."

Charles Fox laughed when he heard it. But he was serious when he came to speak of Chartersea, and bade me look out for assassination. I had Banks follow me abroad at night with a brace of pistols under his coat, albeit I feared nothing save that I should not have an opportunity to meet the duke in a fair fight. And I resolved at all hazards to run Mr. Marmaduke down with despatch, if I had to waylay him.

Mr. Storer, who was forever giving parties, was responsible for this one at Vauxhall. We went in three coaches, and besides Dorothy and Mr. Marmaduke, the company included Lord and Lady Carlisle, Sir Charles and Lady Sarah Bunbury, Lady Ossory and Lady Julia Howard, two Miss Stanleys and Miss Poole, and Comyn, and Hare, and Price, and Fitzpatrick, the latter feeling very glum over a sum he had dropped that afternoon to Lord Harrington. Fox had been called to St. Stephen's on more printer's business.

Dolly was in glowing pink, as I loved best to see her, and looked divine. Comyn and I were in Mr. Manners's coach. The evening was fine and warm, and my lady in very lively spirits. As we rattled over Westminster Bridge, the music of the Vauxhall band came "throbbing through the still night," and the sky was bright with the reflection of the lights. It was the fashion with the quality to go late; and so eleven o'clock had struck before we had pulled up between Vauxhall stairs, crowded with watermen and rough mudlarks, and the very ordinary-looking house which forms the entrance of the great garden. Leaving the servants outside, single-file we trailed through the dark passage guarded by the wicketgate.

"Prepare to be ravished, Richard," said my lady, with fine sarcasm.

"You were yourself born in the colonies, miss," I retorted. "I confess to a thrill, and will not pretend that I have seen such sights often enough to be sated."

"La!" exclaimed Lady Sarah, who had overheard; "I vow this is refreshing.
Behold a new heaven and a new earth, Mr. Carvel?"

Indeed, much to the amusement of the company, I took no pains to hide my enthusiasm at the brilliancy of the scene which burst upon me. A great orchestra rose in the midst of a stately grove lined on all four sides with supper-boxes of brave colours, which ran in straight tiers or swept around in circles. These were filled with people of all sorts and conditions, supping and making merry. Other people were sauntering under the trees, keeping step with the music. Lamps of white and blue and red and green hung like luminous fruit from the branches, or clustered in stars and crescents upon the buildings.

"Why, Richard, you are as bad as Farmer Colin."

> "'O Patty! Soft in feature,
> I've been at dear Vauxhall;
> No paradise is sweeter,
> Not that they Eden call.'"

whispered Dolly, paraphrasing.

At that instant came hurrying Mr. Tom Tyers, who was one of the brothers, proprietors of the gardens. He was a very lively young fellow who seemed to know everybody, and he desired to know if we would walk about a little before being shown to the boxes reserved for us.

"They are on the right side, Mr. Tyers?" demanded Mr. Storer.

"Oh, to be sure, sir. Your man was most particular to stipulate the pink and blue flowered brocades, next the Prince of Wales's."

"But you must have the band stop that piece, Mr. Tyers," cried Lady Sarah. "I declare, it is too much for my nerves. Let them play Dibbin's Ephesian Matron."

"As your Ladyship wishes," responded the

obliging Mr. Tyers, and sent off an uniformed warder to the band-master.

As he led us into the Rotunda, my Lady Dolly, being in one of her whimsical humours, began to recite in the manner of the guide-book, to the vast diversion of our party and the honest citizens gaping at us.

"This, my lords, ladies, and gentlemen," says the minx, "is that marvellous Rotunda commonly known as the 'umbrella,' where the music plays on wet nights, and where we have our masquerades and ridottos. Their Royal Highnesses are very commonly seen here on such occasions. As you see, it is decorated with mirrors and scenes and busts, and with gilded festoons. That picture was painted by the famous Hogarth. The organ in the orchestra cost—you must supply the figure, Mr. Tyers,—and the ceiling is at least two hundred feet high. Gentlemen from the colonies and the country take notice."

By this time we were surrounded. Mr. Marmaduke was scandalized and crushed, but Mr. Tyers, used to the vagaries of his fashionable patrons, was wholly convulsed.

"Faith, Miss Manners, and you would consent to do this two nights more, we should have to open another gate," he declared. Followed by the mob, which it seems was part of the excitement, he led us out of the building into the Grand Walk; and offered to turn on the waterfall and mill, which (so Lady Sarah explained to me) the farmers and merchants fell down and worshipped every night at nine, to the tinkling of bells. She told Mr. Tyers there was diversion enough without "tin cascades." When we got to the Grand Cross Walk he pointed out the black "Wilderness" of tall elms and cedars looming ahead of us. And—so we came to the South Walk, with its three triumphal arches framing a noble view of architecture at the far end. Our gentlemen sauntered ahead, with their spy-glasses, staring the citizens' pretty daughters out of countenance, and making cynical remarks.

"Why, egad!" I heard Sir Charles say, "the wig-makers have no cause to petition his Majesty for work. I'll be sworn the false hair this good staymaker has on cost a guinea."

A remark which caused the staymaker (if such he was) such huge discomfort that he made off with his wife in the opposite direction, to the time of jeers and cock-crows from the bevy of Vauxhall bucks walking abreast.

"You must show us the famous 'dark walks,' Mr. Tyers," says Dorothy.

"Surely you will not care to see those, Miss Manners."

"O lud, of course you must," chimed in the Miss Stanleys; "there is no spice in these flaps and flies."

He led us accordingly into Druid's Walk, overarched with elms, and dark as the shades, our gentlemen singing, "'Ods! Lovers will contrive,'" in chorus, the ladies exclaiming and drawing together. Then I felt a soft, restraining hold on my arm, and fell back instinctively, vibrating to the touch.

"Could you not see that I have been trying to get a word with you for ever so long?"

"I trust you to find a way, Dolly, if you but wish," I replied, admiring her stratagem.

"I am serious to-night." Indeed, her voice betrayed as much. How well I recall those rich and low tones! "I said I wished you shut up in the Marshalsea, and I meant it. I have been worrying about you."

"You make me very happy," said I; which was no lie.

"Richard, you are every bit as reckless and indifferent of danger as they say your father was. And I am afraid—"

"Of what?" I asked quickly.

"You once mentioned a name to me—"

"Yes?" I was breathing deep.

"I have forgiven you," she said gently. "I never meant to have referred to that incident more. You will understand whom I mean. You must know that he is a dangerous man, and a treacherous. Oh!" she exclaimed, "I have been in hourly terror ever since you rode against him in Hyde Park. There! I have said it."

The tense sweetness of that moment none will ever know.

"But you have more reason to fear him than I, Dorothy."

"Hush!" she whispered, catching her breath; "what are you saying?"

"That he has more cause to fear me than I to dread him."

She came a little closer.

"You stayed in London for me, Richard. Why did you? There was no need," she exclaimed; "there was no need, do you hear? Oh, I shall never forgive Comyn for his meddling! I am sure 'twas he who told you some ridiculous story. He had no foundation for it."

"Dorothy," I demanded, my voice shaking with earnestness, "will you tell me honestly there is no foundation for the report that the duke is intriguing to marry you?"

That question was not answered, and regret came the instant it had left my lips—regret and conviction both. Dorothy joined Lady Carlisle before our absence had been noted, and began to banter Fitzpatrick upon his losings.

We were in the lighted Grove again, and sitting down to a supper of Vauxhall fare: transparent slices of ham (which had been a Vauxhall joke for ages), and chickens and cheese cakes and champagne and claret, and arrack punch. Mr. Tyers extended the concert in our favour. Mrs. Weichsell and the beautiful Baddeley trilled sentimental ballads which our ladies chose; and Mr. Vernon, the celebrated tenor, sang Cupid's Recruiting Sergeant so happily that Storer sent him a bottle of champagne. After which we amused ourselves with catches until the space between our boxes and the orchestra was filled. In the midst of this Comyn came quietly in from the other box and took a seat beside me.

"Chartersea is here to-night," said he.

I started. "How do you know?"

"Tyers told me he turned up half an hour since. Tom asked his Grace to join our party," his Lordship laughed. "Duke said no—he was to be here only half an hour, and Tom did not push him. He told me as a joke, and thinks Chartersea came to meet some petite."

"Any one with him?" I asked.

"Yes. Tall, dark man, one eye cast,—that's Lewis. They have come on some dirty work, Richard. Watch little Marmaduke. He has been fidgety as a cat all night."

"That's true," said I. Looking up, I caught Dorothy's eyes upon us, her lips parted, uneasiness and apprehension plain upon her face. Comyn dropped his voice still lower.

"I believe she suspects something," he said, rising. "Chartersea is gone off toward the Wilderness, so Tom says. You must not let little Marmaduke see him. If Manners gets up to go, I will tune up Black-eked reasonable time, I'll after you."

He had been gone scant three minutes before I heard his clear voice singing, "in the Downs", and up I got, with a precipitation far from politic, and stepped out of the box. Our company stared in surprise. But Dorothy rose clear from her chair. The terror I saw stamped upon her face haunts me yet, and I heard her call my name.

I waited for nothing. Gaining the Grand Walk, I saw Mr. Marmaduke's insignificant figure dodging fearfully among the roughs, whose hour it was. He traversed the Cross Walk, and twenty yards farther on dived into an opening in the high hedge bounding the Wilderness. Before he had made six paces I had him by the shoulder, and he let out a shriek of fright like a woman's.

"It is I, Richard Carvel, Mr. Manners," I said shortly. I could not keep out the contempt from my tone. "I beg a word with you."

In his condition then words were impossible. His teeth rattled again, and he trembled like a hare caught alive. I kept my hold of him, and employed the time until he should be more composed peering into the darkness. For all I knew Chartersea might be within ear-shot. But I could see nothing but black trunks of trees.

"What is it, Richard?"

"You are going to meet Chartersea," I said.

He must have seen the futility of a lie, or else was scared out of all contrivance. "Yes," he said weakly.

"You have allowed it to become the talk of London that this filthy nobleman is blackmailing you for your daughter," I went on, without wasting words. "Tell me, is it, or is it not, true?"

As he did not answer, I retained a handful of the grained silk on his shoulder as a measure of precaution.

"Is this so?" I repeated.

"You must know, I suppose," he said, under his breath, and with a note of sullenness.

"I must," I said firmly. "The knowledge is the weapon need, for I, too, am going to meet Chartersea."

He ceased quivering all at once.

"You are going to meet him!" he cried, in another voice. "Yes, yes, it is so,—it is so. I will tell you all."

"Keep it to yourself, Mr. Manners," I replied,

with repugnance, "I have heard all I wish. Where is he?" I demanded.

"Hold the path until you come to him. And God bless—"

I shook my head.

"No, not that! Do you go back to the company and make some excuse for me. Do not alarm them. And if you get the chance, tell Lord Comyn where to come."

I waited until I saw him under the lights of the Grand Walk, and fairly running. Then I swung on my heel. I was of two minds whether to wait for Comyn, by far the wiser course. The unthinking recklessness I had inherited drove me on.

CHAPTER XLI

THE WILDERNESS

My eyes had become accustomed to the darkness, and presently I made out a bench ahead, with two black figures starting from it. One I should have known on the banks of the Styx. From each came a separate oath as I stopped abreast them, and called the duke by name.

"Mr. Carvel!" he cried; "what the devil do you here, sir?"

"I am come to keep an appointment for Mr. Manners," I said. "May I speak to your Grace alone?"

He made a peculiar sound by sucking in his breath, meant for a sneering laugh.

"No," says he, "damned if you shall! I have nothing in common with you, sir. So love for Miss Manners has driven you mad, my young upstart. And he is not the first, Lewis."

"Nor the last, by G——," says the captain.

"I have a score to settle with you, d——n you!" cried Chartersea.

"That is why I am here, your Grace," I replied; "only you have twisted the words. There has been foul play enough. I have come to tell you," I cried, boiling with anger, "I have come to tell you there has been foul play enough with a weakling that cannot protect himself, and to put an end to your blackmail."

In the place of an oath, a hoarse laugh of derision came out of him. But I was too angry then to note its significance. I slapped his face—nay, boxed it so that my palm stung. I heard his sword scraping out of the scabbard, and drew mine, stepping back to distance at the same instant. Then, with something of a shudder, I remembered young Atwater, and a 380 brace of other instances of his villany. I looked for the captain. He was gone.

Our blades, the duke's and mine, came together with a ring, and I felt the strength of his wrist behind his, and of his short, powerful arm. The steel sung with our quick changes from 'quarte' to 'tierce'. 'Twas all by the feeling, without light to go by, and hatred between us left little space for skill. Our lunges were furious. 'Twas not long before I felt his point at my chest, but his reach was scant. All at once the music swelled up voices and laughter were wafted faintly from the pleasure world of lights beyond. But my head was filled, to the exclusion of all else, with a hatred and fury. And (God forgive me!) from between my teeth came a prayer that if I might kill this monster, I would die willingly.

Suddenly, as I pressed him, he shifted ground, and there was Lewis standing within range of my eye. His hands were nowhere—they were behind his back! God alone knows why he had not murdered me. To keep Chartersea between him and me I swung another quarter. The duke seemed to see my game, struggled against it, tried to rush in under my guard, made a vicious lunge that would have ended me then and there had he not slipped. We were both panting like wild beasts. When next I raised my eyes Lewis had faded into the darkness. Then I felt my head as wet as from a plunge, the water running on my brow, and my back twitching. Every second I thought the sting of his sword was between my ribs. But to forsake the duke would have been the maddest of follies.

In that moment of agony came footsteps beating on the path, and by tacit consent our swords were still. We listened.

"Richard! Richard Carvel!"

For the second time in my life I thanked Heaven for that brave and loyal

English heart. I called back, but my throat was dry

and choked.

"So they are at their d——d assassins' tricks again! You need have no fear of one murderer."

With that their steels rang out behind me, like broadswords, Lewis wasting his breath in curses and blasphemies. I began to push Chartersea with all my might, and the wonder of it was that we did not fight with our fingers on each other's necks. His attacks, too, redoubled. Twice I felt the stings of his point, once in the hand, and once in the body, but I minded them as little as pinpricks. I was sure I had touched him, too. I heard him blowing distressedly. The casks of wine he had drunk in his short life were telling now, and his thrusts grew weaker. That fiercest of all joys—of killing an enemy—was in me, when I heard a cry that rang in my ears for many a year afterward, and the thud of a body on the ground.

"I have done for him, your Grace," says Lewis, with an oath; and added immediately, "I think I hear people."

Before I had reached my Lord the captain repeated this, and excitedly begged the duke, I believe, to fly. Chartersea hissed out that he would not move a step until he had finished me, and as I bent over the body his point popped through my coat, and the pain shot under my shoulder. I staggered, and fell. A second of silence ensued, when the duke said with a laugh that was a cackle:

"He won't marry her, d——n him!" (panting). "He had me cursed near killed, Lewis. Best give him another for luck."

I felt his heavy hand on the sword, and it

tearing out of me. Next came the single word "Dover," and they were gone. I had not lost my senses, and was on my knees again immediately, ripping open Comyn's waistcoat with my left hand, and murmuring his name in an agony of sorrow. I was searching under his shirt, wet with blood, when I became aware of voices at my side. "A duel! A murder! Call the warders! Warders, ho!"

"A surgeon!" I cried. "A surgeon first of all!"

Some one had wrenched a lamp from the Grand Walk and held it, flickering in the wind, before his Lordship's face. Guided by its light, more people came running through the wood, then the warders with lanthorns, headed by Mr. Tyers, and on top of him Mr. Fitzpatrick and my Lord Carlisle. We carried poor Jack to the house at the gate, and closed the doors against the crowd.

By the grace of Heaven Sir Charles Blicke was walking in the gardens that night, and, battering at the door, was admitted along with the constable and the watch. Assisted by a young apothecary, Sir Charles washed and dressed the wound, which was in the left groin, and to our anxious questions replied that there was a chance of recovery.

"But you, too, are hurt, sir," he said, turning his clear eyes upon me. Indeed, the blood had been dripping from my hand and arm during the whole of the operation, and I began to be weak from the loss of it. By great good fortune Chartersea's thrust, which he thought had ended my life, passed under my armpit from behind and, stitching the skin, lodged deep in my right nipple. This wound the surgeon bound carefully, and likewise two smaller ones.

The constable was for carrying me to the Marshalsea. And so I was forced to tell that I had quarrelled with Chartersea; and the watch, going out to the scene of the fight, discovered the duke's sword which he had pulled out of me, and Lewis's laced hat; and also a trail of blood leading from the spot. Mr. Tyers testified that he had seen Chartersea that night, and Lord Carlisle and Fitzpatrick to the grudge the duke bore me. I was given my liberty.

Comyn was taken to his house in Brook Street, Grosvenor Square, in Sir Charles's coach, whither I insisted upon preceding him. 'Twas on the way there that Fitzpatrick told me Dorothy had fainted when she heard the alarm—a piece of news which added to my anxiety. We called up the dowager countess, Comyn's mother, and Carlisle broke the news to her, mercifully lightening me of a share of the blame. Her Ladyship received the tidings with great fortitude; and instead of the torrent of reproaches I looked for, and deserved, she implored me to go home and care for my injuries lest I get the fever. I believe that I burst into tears.

His Lordship was carried up the stairs with never a word or a groan from his lips, and his heart beating out slowly.

We reached my lodgings as the watchman was crying: "Past two o'clock, and a windy morning!"

Mr. Fitzpatrick stayed with me that night. And the next morning, save for the soreness of the cuts I had got, I found myself well as ever. I was again to thank the robustness of my health. Despite the protests of Banks and Fitzpatrick, and of Mr. Fox (who arrived early, not having been to bed at all), I jumped into a chaise and drove to Brook Street. There I had the good fortune to get the greatest load from my mind. Comyn was resting so much easier that the surgeon had left, and her Ladyship retired two hours since.

The day was misting and dark, but so vast was my relief that I imagined the sun was out as I rattled toward Arlington Street. If only Dolly were not ill again from the shock, I should be happy indeed. She must have heard, ere then, that I was not killed; and I had still better news to tell her than that of Lord Comyn's condition. Mr. Fox, who got every rumour that ran, had shouted after me that the duke and Lewis were set out for France. How he knew I had not waited to inquire. But the report tallied with my own surmise, for they had used the word "Dover" when they left us for dead in the Wilderness.

I dismissed my chaise at the door.

"Mr. Manners waits on you, sir, in the drawing-room," said the footman.
"Your honour is here sooner than he looked for," he added gratuitously.

"Sooner than he looked for?"

"Yes, sir. James is gone to you but quarter of an hour since with a message, sir."

I was puzzled.

"And Miss Manners? Is she well?"

The man smiled.

"Very well, sir, thank your honour."

To add to my surprise, Mr. Marmaduke was pacing the drawing-room in a yellow night-gown.

He met me with an expression I failed to fathom, and then my eye was held by a letter in his hand. He cleared his throat.

"Good morning, Richard," said he, very serious,—very pompous, I thought. "I am pleased to see that you are so well out of the deplorable affair of last night."

I had not looked for gratitude. In truth, I had done nothing for him, and Chartersea might have exposed him a highwayman for all I cared,—I had fought for Dolly. But this attitude astonished me. I was about to make a tart reply, and then thought better of it.

"Walter, a decanter of wine for Mr. Carvel," says he to the footman.
Then to me: "I am rejoiced to hear that Lord Comyn is out of danger."

I merely stared at him.

"Will you sit?" he continued. "To speak truth, the Annapolis packet came in last night with news for you. Knowing that you have not had time to hear from Maryland, I sent for you."

My brain was in such a state that for the moment I took no meaning from this introduction. I was conscious only of indignation against him for sending for me, when for all he knew I might have been unable to leave my bed. Suddenly I jumped from the chair.

"You have heard from Maryland?" I cried. "Is Mr. Carvel dead? Oh, tell me, is Mr. Carvel dead?" And I clutched his arm to make him wince.

He nodded, and turned away. "My dear old friend is no more," he said.

"Your grandfather passed away on the seventh of last month."

I sank into a chair and bowed my face, a flood of recollections overwhelming me, a thousand kindnesses of my grandfather coming to mind. One comfort alone stood forth, even had I gone home with John Paul, I had missed him. But that he should have died alone with Grafton brought the tears brimming to my eyes. I had thought to be there to receive his last words and blessing, to watch over him, and to Smooth his pillow. Who had he else in the world to bear him affection on his death-bed? The imagination of that scene drove me mad.

Mr. Manners aroused me by a touch, and I looked up quickly. So quickly that I surprised the trace of a smile about his weak mouth. Were I to die to-morrow, I would swear to this on the Evangels. Nor was it the smile which compels itself upon the weak in serious moments. Nay, there was in it something malicious. And Mr. Manners could not even act.

"There is morc, Richard," he was saying; "there is worse to come. Can you bear it?"

His words and look roused me from my sorrow. I have ever been short of temper with those I disliked, and (alas!) with my friends also. And now all my pent-up wrath against this little man broke forth. I divined his meaning, and forgot that he was Dorothy's father.

"Worse?" I shouted, while he gave back in his alarm. "Do you mean that Grafton has got possession of the estate? Is that what you mean, sir?"

"Yes," he gasped, "yes. I pray you be calm."

"And you call that worse than losing my dearest friend on earth?" I cried. There must have been an infinite scorn in my voice. "Then your standards and mine are different, Mr. Manners. Your ways and mine are different, and I thank God for it. You have played more than one double part with me. You looked me in the face and denied me, and left me to go to a prison. I shall not repeat my grandfather's kindnesses to you, sir. Though you may not recall them, I do. And if your treatment of me was known in Maryland, you would be drummed out of the colony even as Mr. Hood was, and hung in effigy"

"As God hears me, Richard—"

"Do not add perjury to it," I said. "And have no uneasiness that I shall publish you. Your wife and daughter have saved you before,—they will save you now."

I paused, struck speechless by a suspicion that suddenly flashed into my head. A glance at the contemptible form cowering within the folds of the flowered gown clinched it to a conviction. In two strides I had seized him by the skin over his ribs, and he shrieked with pain and fright.

"You—you snake!" I cried, in uncontrollable anger. "You well knew Dorothy's spirit, which she has not got from you, and you lied to her. Yes, lied, I say. To force her to marry Chartersea you made her believe that your precious honour was in danger. And you lied to me last night, and sent me in the dark to fight two of the most treacherous villains in England. You wish they had killed me. The plot was between you and his Grace. You, who have not a cat's courage, commit an indiscretion! You never made one in your life, Tell me," I cried, shaking him until his teeth smote together, "was it not put up between you?"

"Let me go! Let me go, and I will tell!" he wailed in the agony of my grip. I tightened it the more.

"You shall confess it first," I said, from between my teeth.

Scarce had his lips formed the word yes, when I had flung him half across the room. He tripped on his gown, and fell sprawling on his hands. So the servant found us when he came back with the tray. The lackey went out again hastily.

"My God!" I exclaimed, in bitterness and disgust; "you are a father, and would sell both your daughter and your honour for a title, and to the filthiest wretch in the kingdom?"

Without bestowing upon him another look, I turned on my heel and left the room. I had set my foot on the stair, when I heard the rustle of a dress, and the low voice which I knew so well calling my name.

"Richard."

There at my side was Dorothy, even taller in her paleness, with sorrow and agitation in her blue eyes.

"Richard, I have heard all.—I listened. Are you going away without a word for me?" Her breath came fast, and mine, as she laid a hand upon my arm. "Richard, I do not care whether you are poor.

What am I saying?" she cried wildly. "Am I false to my own father? Richard, what have you done?"

And then, while I stood dazed, she tore open her gown, and drawing forth a little gold locket, pressed it in my palm. "The flowers you gave me on your birthday,—the lilies of the valley, do you remember? They are here, Richard. I have worn them upon my heart ever since."

I raised the locket to my lips.

"I shall treasure it for your sake, Dorothy," I said, "for the sake of the old days. God keep you!"

For a moment I looked into the depths of her eyes. Then she was gone, and I went down the stairs alone. Outside, the rain fell unheeded on my new coat. My steps bent southward, past Whitehall, where the martyr Charles had met death so nobly: past the stairs to the river, where she had tripped with me so gayly not a month since. Death was in my soul that day,—death and love, which is the mystery of life. God guided me into the great Abbey near by, where I fell on my knees before Him and before England's dead. He had raised them and cast them down, even as He was casting me, that I might come to know the glory of His holy name.

END OF Ashed Phoenix Library'S RICHARD CARVEL, VOLUME 6, BY WINSTON CHURCHILL

9 780368 282898